AFTER THE DARK

SAMANTHA HICKS

ALSO BY SAMANTHA HICKS

Trusting Hearts

AFTER THE DARK

SAMANTHA HICKS

Affinity
Rainbow Publications

2019

After the Dark
© 2018 by Samantha Hicks

Affinity E-Book Press NZ LTD
Canterbury, New Zealand

1st Edition

ISBN: 978-1-98-854989-7

Editor: Angela Koenig
Proof Editor: Alexis Smith
Cover Design: Irish Dragon Design
Production Design: Affinity Publication Services

ACKNOWLEDGMENTS

It has been a lifelong dream of mine to be a published author and it's bizarre for the dream to now be my reality.

Once again, my utmost thanks and gratitude goes to the lovely ladies at Affinity Rainbow Publications. Mel, Julie, and Nancy have been invaluable in this process and I have learned so much from this talented bunch and I truly appreciate all their hard work and brilliance in making this book what it is today. I couldn't imagine doing this without them and hope to continue working with them for a long time to come.

I want to thank my family for supporting me through all this, and especially to Lyndsey and Josh who spoil me with pizza, wine, and chocolate (my favourite things). A huge thank you goes to my constant companion Finley, my springer spaniel, who allows me the time to write and makes me go outside in the fresh air to walk him. There is no better writing partner than a dog. And thank you, Kelly, for allowing me the use of your surname, welcome to the family.

My appreciation goes to all the staff at Affinity for their dedication in making all our books sparkle. And finally, thank you to all the readers and writers I have connected with over the last year. It's a wonderful community and I'm honoured to be a part of it.

DEDICATION

To Sam Jones,

You truly are the world's most generous man \and my lifelong friend.

Thank you for everything.

TABLE OF CONTENTS

CHAPTER ONE

"Don't forget we're meeting Ted and Wendy at seven o'clock tonight, darling."

"Yeah, I remember, Kath. I should be back by five, at the latest, so I'll have plenty of time to get ready." Meredith took her eyes off the country road in front of her, flicking her gaze over the GPS sitting on her dashboard. Shaking her head, she muttered, "This is ridiculous."

"Sorry, honey, I didn't get that," her long-term partner Kathleen said from the speakerphone.

Stop with all the bloody cutesy names! Meredith hated the pet names. She marvelled at how many Kathleen knew, hardly ever the same one twice. She wasn't sure if she hated them in general or if it was just Kathleen's use of them that irritated her. She pulled her gaze back to the winding road.

"I was talking to the GPS. I'm sure the guy at the car dealership messed with the programming just to mess with me." She remembered the look in his eyes, the smarmy way he leered at her. She had been brusque with him, hoping he'd take the hint that she wasn't interested. He did, and she was positive he did this to her GPS because it was the fifth time in two weeks, she had gotten lost following its directions.

"Sweetheart, are you sure you'll be back in time?"

Meredith was on her way to meet a client in the Yorkshire Dales, and as she was driving up from Bristol, she had been on the road since six that morning. The meeting would be relatively quick, so she had plenty of time to get back home. She had originally tried putting Kathleen off from meeting her friends, knowing she would be tired after driving most of the day, but Kathleen wouldn't hear of it. Ted and Wendy were not the kinds of people you put off, apparently.

Meredith rolled her eyes at Kathleen's whining tone. "Yes, I'll be back in time, I promise." No sooner as she uttered those words when an ominous, loud, grumbling sound came from the front left tire. She quickly said her goodbyes and slowed to a stop in the middle of the narrow country lane.

She pulled on the handbrake, switched off the engine, and got out of her newly leased BMW Seven Series car. The wind blew softly around her, and she reached up to push the fire-cracker-red curls back from her face. She bent low and examined the now flat tire, cursing under her breath that she had never allowed her father to teach her how to change one. Just as she stood up with the intent of calling her breakdown service, she caught the flash of something big and heavy swinging toward her face, catching her on her right temple.

Pain exploded in her head, her gaze swam out of focus. Landing on her back, she caught sight of a dark figure leaning into view. She had the tiniest glimpse of soulless eyes staring into hers. Glove-covered hands reached for her, and before Meredith had the chance to scream, her world went black.

†

Meredith awoke in pure darkness. She lay on a thin, ratty, and smelly mattress. As far as she could tell she was alone. Her eyes adjusted to the inky black surroundings but still couldn't make out any form or function to the room. It was small, she thought she could see a door to her left. As she tried to stand, her arm snapped back behind her, her wrist tied to something by a chain, keeping her in place.

She sank back into the filthy mattress, trying to piece together what had happened, how long she had been here. Meredith had no idea about anything. The handful of times she had awakened it had been to the sounds of the Man shouting at her as he humiliated her and abused her. Her body was bruised and damaged, she had no clue as to how many times he had beaten her, raped her, or tortured her.

Meredith ran her swollen hand through her thick, matted hair, realising she hadn't had a bath in God knows how long. She smelt horrid. If Kathleen could see me now, she mused. She wondered if Kathleen was all right, if she was worried about her, looking for her. Surely someone had found her car by now. Not if the man took it with him! There was a good chance no one had any idea where to even look for her. Kathleen only knew the general area Meredith had travelled to, not the exact location of the meeting. She hadn't been overly interested where Meredith was going, only that she be back in time to meet her friends. Meredith had the sardonic thought that maybe being here wasn't all that bad if it meant missing out on meeting with Ted and Wendy.

Meredith continued to think about her circumstances, trying to find a bit of hope in an otherwise impossible situation. She had just about given up on planning her escape when the door to her left flew open. The Man walked over to her and kicked her hard in the leg. Pain exploded in her thigh. Her whole body ached, not one part of her felt normal. It wouldn't have mattered where he kicked her, she still would have felt the pain all through herself.

"You dead yet? You've lasted longer than the others." He pulled her up by her hair and twisted her around to unlock the cuff on her wrist. "Don't be stupid, bitch," he warned.

"How long have I been here?" He didn't reply. "Look, I'm sure I can get you money, I'm a wealthy woman. I know people." She tried all she could to talk to him as he pulled her down a darkened hallway, her feet dragging along the stone floor, skin peeling off as she tried to push back away from him.

He opened a door at the end after a thirty-second walk from her previous location. She counted at least ten other doors on either side of the corridor and she prayed they didn't conceal any other victims. He did say I outlasted the others, perhaps there were dead women in them. Horrified at the thought, she began to struggle against his grip. He backhanded her across the cheek and roughly threw her down onto the hard concrete floor, the rough stone cutting into her back. The air was decidedly chillier in here and it raised gooseflesh on her overheated skin.

"Time for some more fun." He punched her in the face and she was momentarily stunned, blinking her eyes, trying to clear the pinpoints of light dancing in her gaze. This gave him enough time to tie her down in the shackles spread out on the floor. Lying there, spread eagle, Meredith felt her emotions shutting down. This room was new. She couldn't remember being in here before, unless she had been unconscious, and she feared what would happen to her now. Closing herself off on the inside was the only way she could get through whatever was about to happen. If she thought too much about it, it would drive her insane. Putting her mind to a place of happier times she thought of her childhood, her old bedroom, and her parents. She thought of anything she could to remove herself away from the brutality he was about to inflict on her and the tightness of the shackles around her extremities.

He injected something into her arm and slowly her tense muscles began to relax. She couldn't move, her eyes refused to remain open. Her last recollection was of her dirty blouse being ripped from her skin.

CHAPTER TWO

"Make yourself comfortable, you're going to be here a while," the man said.

Meredith felt a warm body press close to her, and she caught a faint whiff of roses, probably from her perfume, mixed with a strong smell of alcohol. She listened to the sound of the door slamming shut, then she opened her eyes to see the bruised and bloodied face of a woman in front of her, her dark hair falling across her cheek. She sympathised with this new person, and she faintly recalled how she had felt when she first awoke in this nightmare.

Gently she smoothed the soft hair back from the woman's face, assessing the cut above the newcomer's eye. Pain-filled dark-green eyes blinked back at her.

"Hey," Meredith whispered.

"Who are you? Where am I?"

Meredith concentrated on staying awake. She hadn't eaten for so long that her energy was all but gone. He only fed her a small, stale bread roll every few days and she couldn't remember when the last time that had been.

"My name is Meredith and we're in hell."

The newcomer closed her eyes; all her energy appeared to drain out of her. With her lashes still lowered, she murmured, "How long have you been here?"

Meredith didn't know. It felt like a lifetime. She asked the woman what the date was, and she was shocked to learn, once she calculated back to the date she was taken, she had been here nearly seven months.

"Seven months," she said wearily. She had missed Christmas. She had missed her birthday. Her periods had stopped weeks ago, and she knew her system was failing. She wouldn't be alive much longer. She gave up all hope of ever getting out.

The woman's eyes snapped open and a tear tumbled down her cheek. Meredith used her thumb to wipe it away, dismayed that she herself couldn't conjure any tears anymore. Seven months in this hell would do that to you, I suppose.

"I'm sorry," The woman said softly. "We probably aren't getting out of here, are we?"

"No, I don't think so." Meredith removed her hand and rolled onto her back, staring up into the darkness. "What's your name?" she asked quietly.

"Stephanie. Stephanie Edwards."

"It's nice to meet you, Stephanie. I'm not sure what to say to you. Things are going to happen to you that I wish you didn't have to go through, but there is nothing you or I can do to stop him. He's had me here for seven fucking months!"

Stephanie reached her hand out toward Meredith's and closed warm fingers over her tight fist. A few moments later, Meredith relaxed her hand and they laced their fingers together.

"I don't know how you've lasted all this time, but you have," Stephanie whispered. "I can only imagine what has happened to you and I'm sorry. But you're obviously a strong person to have survived this long. We'll get out of here, I'm sure of it."

Meredith felt Stephanie's head rest gently against her shoulder and she drifted off to sleep still holding her hand. She felt oddly comforted by this stranger, and she prayed both would somehow survive. She was kidding herself, she knew. It would only be a matter of time before her body shut down completely.

It wasn't long, it only felt like a few minutes to Meredith before she was startled awake by movement in the room. The Man grabbed Stephanie from beside her and dragged her toward the door. She could see Stephanie struggle in his grip and she shouted at him to stop. Meredith tried to reach for her, but she couldn't stretch far enough. The cuff at her wrist cut into her skin as she struggled to reach for Stephanie.

"Leave her alone, you freak!" she shouted and screamed at him, but he didn't respond. He ignored her pleas as if she wasn't even there. The slamming of the door and the fading shouts of Stephanie ended her struggle to release herself from her restraint. Her wrist, bloodied from her effort to escape, throbbed, and she sat back against the cold wall, cradling her hand in her lap. She closed her eyes, trying to block out the images plaguing her mind, knowing what that bastard was going to do to Stephanie.

Meredith had been there, she knew the perverse pleasure the man took in torturing her, abusing her. She hoped, for Stephanie's sake, that he would be quick today. That he wouldn't hurt her for too long. He seemed to have no problem in keeping at it for hours at a time. The torment he inflicted on Meredith appeared to spur him on more and more and he never tired, never exhausted himself. She wondered what level of psychosis he was in because, clearly, he was a psychopath.

†

"Tell me about yourself," Stephanie murmured.

"What do you want to know?"

They were sitting side by side, backs up against the wall. Meredith guessed Stephanie had now been here three days. Three days of intermittent torture for them both. The man didn't appear to stick to any schedule and Meredith wondered if he had a job, if he was a member of society, or if he just spent all his time torturing women.

She still hadn't seen or heard any other people, but she supposed there were others. It seemed logical that, if he had the two of them, there were more. Perhaps the rooms are soundproofed?

"I don't know, anything. Are you married?"

Meredith closed her eyes and Kathleen's face drifted into focus.

"Not married, no. But I do have a partner, Kathleen." She sensed Stephanie's gaze on her and wondered about her reaction. Meredith had never been closeted and she wasn't ashamed of who she was, even if others had a problem with it. And besides, with where they were now and the likelihood of their death in this place, it didn't really matter what Stephanie thought of her.

"You're gay?"

"Yes."

"Cool."

Stephanie shifted on the mattress and faced Meredith fully.

"What's she like?"

"Not much to tell. Her name is Kathleen. We've been together for four years."

Stephanie waited for more information, but Meredith wasn't eager to talk.

"Is that it? Come on; tell me what she's like."

Meredith thought for a moment, trying to sum up Kathleen in a few sentences. The truth was there wasn't much Meredith could say about Kathleen. Yes, they had been together a long time, but they didn't really know each other, not properly. They both worked hard, and during their downtime Meredith liked to stay in and catch up on her reading, and Kathleen liked to socialise. If Kathleen couldn't be "seen" by the right people all the time she felt her social standing would slip. They had little in common, but their time together was pleasant. They both found it a mutually respectful and enjoyable relationship.

"She works on the stock exchange, but I'm not entirely sure what she does. She makes a lot of money and that seems to satisfy her." Meredith grew quiet once again, contemplating her relationship, and wondered how Kathleen would cope if she ever got out of this hell. Turning her head toward Stephanie she asked her the same question.

"How about you, married?"

Stephanie snorted. "Not even close. I used to think there was something wrong with me. I've never really had an attraction to anyone, and the times I have had sex I felt detached. It never really did anything for me. Now, what with this happening, I doubt I'll ever have a normal relationship."

Meredith could hear the pain in Stephanie's voice. Gently she took her hand. Changing the subject, as she had no words of comfort to offer, she asked, "How old are you?"

"Twenty-nine."

"You're still a baby."

"I think I've matured pretty much in the last few days."

"Yeah, I know the feeling. I'm forty-one, but I feel dead. I'm not sure how much more of this I can take."

Stephanie started to speak, but the door opening caused them both to jump. They unconsciously moved closer together.

The Man walked in. Meredith couldn't see his face because of the baseball cap he had pulled down low. He wore dark jeans and a stained shirt.

"I'm feeling like revisiting the good ol' days." He stalked over toward them and slapped Stephanie across the face, making her fall back against the wall. He grabbed Meredith, unchained her from the wall, and carried her out of the room.

Meredith didn't even scream. All the fight she had in her had gone days ago. He could do what he wanted, she no longer cared.

†

Freezing water splashed onto Stephanie's face and her eyes flew open. The Man stood at the end of the mattress with a metal bucket in his hand and what looked like old rags in the other. He tossed the rags at Stephanie, put the bucket on the floor, and from the waistband of his jeans he pulled out a small first aid kit.

"I got carried away," he mumbled. "Clean yourselves up and sort out her cuts. I like my meat to be fresh." He turned and left, slamming the door with force.

Stephanie peered into the darkness, seeing Meredith's unconscious form on the mattress next to her. She was naked, and through the dim light, Stephanie could see massive amounts of tiny cuts marring Meredith's torso and breasts.

"Oh, sweetheart, what has he done to you?" she whispered.

Stephanie brought the bucket closer and dunked one of the rags into it. Gently she touched Meredith's face, but there was no reaction. She set about cleaning up the cuts, applying the antiseptic cream the man had given her, and placing plasters where she could. It didn't appear that any cuts needed stitches and Stephanie hoped they wouldn't scar too much.

After she finished the medical care, she began to wash Meredith's body. Getting the months' worth of grime off proved a challenge with only a small amount of water and the now dirty rags. She took off her own shirt and covered Meredith, hoping to provide some form of dignity and comfort for the still unconscious woman.

Stephanie gave herself a quick rub over with the rags and dumped them in the bucket. Settling back, she cradled

Meredith's head in her lap and tenderly stroked her hair, softly humming a nonsensical tune.

†

Meredith opened her eyes and found herself feeling oddly peaceful. It took her a few moments to remember where she was. She became aware of the dull pain radiating over her stomach and chest, but the glide of gentle and strong fingers through her hair settled her.

Stephanie must have sensed Meredith wake up. Her hand stilled, and she murmured a greeting.

"How long have I been out?" Meredith said through cracked, dry lips.

"Not sure, a few hours at least."

Meredith could hear the despondent tone as Stephanie spoke. Stephanie had always had a positive quality in her voice, even after being here for weeks, and Meredith feared she was finally realising they weren't going to get out. Rising, she looked at Stephanie. Her face was closed off, a vacant look in her eyes.

"Hey." She reached up and turned Stephanie's head toward her. "What's the matter?"

"That's a pretty fucking stupid question, don't you think?"

Meredith sucked in a breath at Stephanie's harsh words. She dropped her hand from Stephanie's cheek, the chain restraint attaching her to the wall clattering loudly in the quiet of the room.

"I'm sorry, Meredith, but I'm fucking angry! He cut you up like he wanted to skin you alive! He's doing God-awful things to you, to us, and probably others too. I can't keep doing this."

Meredith pulled her knees to her chest, noticing for the first time she felt cleaner and smelt a little fresher. She became aware of the plasters taped across her wounds. The ratty blouse Stephanie had draped over her fell to the floor.

"Did you do this?" She gestured to herself.

Stephanie's eyes drifted down Meredith's naked form. "Yes. I cleaned you up and fixed your cuts. He gave me some water and a first aid kit. Not sure why he did."

Meredith did cry then. For the first time since she had been taken, she felt her emotions come to the surface. She couldn't bury this feeling if she tried. Warmth spread through her chest and around her body. The Man had never given her anything to clean herself before and certainly not the means to attend to any injuries. She couldn't fathom why he would suddenly start doing this.

"Thank you," Meredith whispered. A tear rolled down her cheek and Stephanie reached out, pulling her into her arms, holding her tightly, while Meredith wept.

†

"Did you hear that?" Meredith asked.

It had been four days since the Man had last been in to hurt either one of them. He had collected the bucket of dirty water not long after Meredith had her crying episode and returned later with a bread roll for each of them and a glass of filthy looking water to share. He hadn't said anything to them, just put the items down and left. He didn't even glance at them.

Every day since then he carried on with the same routine. He'd give them food and water and that was it. Stephanie could only guess as to why he didn't seem interested in them anymore. The loud scream they had heard a moment ago gave her a sick feeling.

"Yeah, I guess there are others down here with us," Stephanie said.

They sat quietly, listening in the dark for any other sounds coming from the corridor. Meredith turned to regard Stephanie.

"Tell me something nice about you. Something fun. Something that can take my mind off this fucking hell-hole."

Stephanie thought for a few moments, trying to remember a time when she at least felt normal. She had never really been happy, just content with who she was and plodding along in life. Now, being here, she could hardly remember the last time she even felt remotely safe.

With no memories coming forward, she shook her head in dismay.

"I can't right now. My head is all messed up. I'm tired, hungry, and can't honestly think of anything I even want to talk about."

Placing a hand on her knee Meredith said, "That's okay, Steph. I just…"

Stephanie cut Meredith off, struck by the fleeting emotion that had just washed through her when Meredith touched her. "I do know that right at this moment I feel safe with you. I know it sounds weird and he could come in at any moment, but I'm happy I'm here with you. I mean, I wish you weren't here, but if we are here, which we are, I'm glad it's with you."

Meredith smiled at her flustering. "Stephanie, it's all right, I know what you mean. I'm glad I'm here with you too."

"Oh, right, I sort of rambled there for a minute, didn't I?"

They smiled softly at each other through the darkness and entwined their fingers together, waiting for the next chapter of this terrifying nightmare to continue.

†

"I've got a bad feeling about this, Meredith."

"I know. Me too."

The Man hadn't been by to feed them in six days. Their strength depleted, they lay side by side, huddled together for warmth. Meredith's lips were cracked, her skin itched like thousands of tiny ants crawling all over her.

"Do you think something has happened to him?"

"Yeah, although I have no clue what. I'm sorry, Steph, that you couldn't get out of here."

Meredith closed her eyes, too tired to talk any more. It took all her energy just to keep breathing. She felt Stephanie shift closer and dry lips gently kissed her forehead.

"It's okay. I never really thought I would anyway."

As they lay there Stephanie began to talk.

"When I was two years old, I was in a car accident. My mum died on impact and I was left with a head injury. I think it hindered my ability to connect with people. I haven't really had many friends and my dad gave me away when he couldn't be bothered to look after me anymore.

"I've always struggled trying to understand other people's thoughts and emotions, I can recognise them, just not understand them. I've never experienced any kind of

16

love. I've been content with life and have a good job working for my only friend, he's more like a brother to me. He's the only person I've ever felt close to."

As she continued to speak, her voice became quieter, the words hard to hear even in the stillness of the room. She whispered tales of the trouble she got into during her school years and how she always felt adrift from everyone else. She spoke of anything, really, to keep the silence of death from creeping up on them.

If they were going to die, Meredith was glad she wouldn't be alone when it happened. And if by some miracle they did survive, she wanted to find out more about Stephanie Edwards.

CHAPTER THREE

The door burst open and the room filled with swaths of torchlight as people rushed in.

A woman shouted, "I've got two more bodies in here," and Meredith felt the warmth of light on her face. She struggled to open her eyes, and as a gentle hand touched the pulse point in her neck, she managed to squint up at the stranger. Shocked eyes regarded her, surprise ghosting across the woman's face.

"Jesus, it smells horrid in here," a second, deep male voice said.

"Get an ambulance here now; we have at least one alive." The woman looked back at Meredith, resting her hand on her shoulder. "It's going to be okay. I'm a police officer. We'll get you out of here soon."

Meredith closed her eyes, trusting the stranger's words. Suddenly remembering Stephanie, her head thrashed to the left, eyes searching Stephanie's face inches from her own.

"Stephanie?" Her voice cracked, Stephanie's name came out in barely a whisper. Stephanie didn't stir.

"We'll look after her, don't worry," the woman said. Her lips set in a grim line, she stretched over Meredith and checked Stephanie's pulse.

At that point two medics walked in, one carrying a backboard and duffel bag, the other pushing a stretcher.

"Check her first," the woman said, pointing at Stephanie's inert body. "I can't find a pulse.

Hearing the words injected Meredith with an uncontrollable rage. She gathered all the strength she could muster and got to her knees. As one medic began CPR and the other started to attach lines and run drugs into Stephanie's arms, Meredith took her hand and ran the fingers of her other hand through Stephanie's filthy hair.

"Come on, Steph, hang on," Meredith whispered fervently. "We're getting out. We're safe."

Stephanie didn't respond. She lay still, the medics trying all they could to breathe life back into her. Finally, the first medic murmured they had a weak pulse. Quickly they slid the backboard under Stephanie, hefted her onto the stretcher, and were gone.

Meredith slumped back onto the soiled and grubby mattress, trembling. The woman took off her flak jacket and draped it over Meredith's shaking body.

"There is another ambulance on the way. We'll get you out of her soon."

A few minutes later, Meredith was being wheeled up the corridor toward the main torture room. Instead of going through there she was taken to a door on the right-hand side. Going through this new darkened hallway, she sensed they were heading uphill.

After a minute of climbing, they broke through into piercing daylight. Meredith closed her eyes at the sudden blinding of the sun. Gradually she adjusted to the new sensation. When she had her eyes open as far as she dared, she was shaken to see four body bags lying next to each other. They were all filled with forms that Meredith assumed were more victims.

Glancing to her right, just before she was lifted into the back of the waiting ambulance, she saw another, younger woman put into a different ambulance. She could hear the hysterical screaming of a different woman. How many of us did he lock up? Sick fucker.

Mercifully, the ambulance door closed behind her and soon they were on their way.

†

Meredith felt familiar fingers running through her hair. She knew that touch, it had comforted her at one time. She opened her eyes, wincing at the bright light that flooded her irises. Once she could fully focus, she saw Kathleen sitting beside her on an uncomfortable looking chair. Meredith took stock of herself. She was exhausted, that much she knew, and her whole body throbbed with the pulse of her heartbeat. She turned her head more fully to face Kathleen.

"Hello."

"Oh, Jesus, sweet pea. I'm so glad you are awake. You've been asleep for four days now. I was beginning to think you would never wake up."

"What happened?"

Kathleen picked up Meredith's hand, laying it gently against her cheek. "The doctors have been running tests on you since you've been here. STDs, blood work, and other things. They think you'll be okay." Kathleen brushed the tears from her eyes.

"I'm sorry."

"Not your fault, darling. I've called your parents and they want to speak to you before they fly back from New York, we have all been so worried about you."

Meredith's energy drained out of her at the mention of her parents. She had missed them terribly and she hoped they were okay. She closed her eyes and drifted back to sleep with the feel of Kathleen's fingers in her hair. Her last conscious thought was wishing Stephanie was here and the feel of Stephanie's fingers touching hers.

†

Meredith woke to the soft voice of the nurse gently calling her back to consciousness. She opened her eyes and blinked to clear the fogginess from them.

"The doctor is on his way to speak to you." The nurse fluffed her pillow and straightened her sheets in a vain attempt to make her feel more comfortable.

A man carrying a clipboard walked in, wearing light-blue scrubs and a pristine-white lab coat. He introduced himself as Dr Carmichael and he did a thorough exam of Meredith. He made a few notes on the papers attached to the clipboard and then turned his gaze to her.

"You are a very lucky woman, Miss Ashcroft. The care you received on your cuts have healed well, and within time, most of them will probably fade with no scarring. We can do laser treatment on the others if that is something you would want in the future. You're severely malnourished, but we have fluids being given and soon, hopefully, we can get you started on solid food."

His eyes shifted around the room, avoiding eye contact as if his next words were unpleasant to speak, and Meredith had a bad feeling about what he was going to say. She mentally prepared herself, thinking that his words would be nothing compared to how much she had already endured.

"We performed a rape kit when you arrived and have taken samples and bloods for testing. Of course, the police have taken some samples as well for evidence. We've done tests for the usual things, HIV, AIDS, hep B and C, et cetera. The results will also take a while to come back, but fingers crossed they will all be negative. We would like to keep you in a couple more days for observation, but barring any unforeseen problems, you can go home."

Meredith blew out a breath. The prospect of home had never occurred to her in the last few months. After the Man had failed to return, she knew she would die. She had made peace with that fact, and although she had been sad for her parents, she herself was okay with it.

The doctor said his farewells and the nurse continued to fuss with her drips as well as checking bandages. Kathleen came back in but avoided eye contact with her. It was as if she was a completely different person from the one, she had been when Meredith had awakened earlier. Something had changed, but Meredith was too tired to try and figure it out. She closed her eyes briefly, then opened them in a panic to search out Kathleen, who had settled in a chair beside her bed.

"Stephanie, is she okay?"

Kathleen looked at her, confused, her brows drawn down, pursing her lips.

"She was with me in the same room," Meredith explained.

"I'm not sure. Would you like me to go and find out for you?"

Meredith nodded, she didn't have the strength to speak. She closed her eyes as Kathleen left the room, her thoughts turning to Stephanie and praying, with everything she had, that she was alive. The possibility of Stephanie dying was unbearable. They had gone through so much together in that place and there was no way Meredith would be able to live with the fact that Stephanie had died and that she had lived. They had bonded in their need to survive and had relied on each other. Meredith was not going to let her down now by believing she could not make it through.

Kathleen came back in a few moments later.

"She's up in ICU, in an induced coma. The doctors have stabilised her, but she nearly didn't make it. They placed her in the coma to give her more time to heal. Hopefully, she should be okay."

Meredith merely nodded, immensely pleased that Stephanie was alive, but with no energy to say anything. She closed her eyes and slept.

CHAPTER FOUR

Stephanie awoke in a haze of white light. Her eyelids slowly fluttered open and she blinked a few times to clear the dryness in them. She felt terrible. Her head thumped in time to her pulse and waves of queasiness rolled through her stomach. She became dimly aware of another person in the room and, for just a second, she was gripped by fear, back in that hell of a basement. She scrunched up her eyes, her muscles tense. She didn't think she could cope with one more vicious thing happening to her.

As the horror in her veins reached fever pitch, she felt a cool hand touch her own, which instantly settled her, soothing her rising panic. She recognised that touch; it had soothed her many times in the last few weeks. Relaxing her body, she turned her head towards Meredith, who sat next to her in a wheelchair.

"Hey." Meredith slowly ran her fingers up and down Stephanie's arm. "I didn't mean to startle you. Are you okay?"

Stephanie opened her eyes fully. She smiled wanly at Meredith.

"Yeah, I'm good. Just for a minute, I was back there."

She shook the last of her fear away and focused on Meredith. She looked a lot better since Stephanie had last seen her. She was clean and fresh but had a haunted look in her eyes with deep shadows encircling them. Her skin was pale, but she was still a beautiful woman. Red hair curled softly around her face and Stephanie had the urge to touch it.

"What happened? I don't remember much since talking to you about my last job."

"I'm not sure of all the details, but I know they caught the guy who did this. Apparently, he tried to abduct another woman, but she got away. Gave a description of him and his car and the police found him. He'd been on the run since the failed attempt, which is why we hadn't seen him for days."

Stephanie frowned. "Were we right, were there others?"

"Including us there were nine other women. Four of whom had died." Meredith grabbed hold of Stephanie's hand when a tear rolled down her cheek.

"We survived. We got out, just like you promised we would."

"I'm sorry; I just can't believe anyone would do this to other human beings. What a sick fucker."

"Now you're awake, I imagine the police will come by to speak to you."

"You'll be here, right? I don't want to talk to them alone." Stephanie could see the regret in Meredith's eyes before she even uttered the words.

"I'm sorry, but I'm heading back to Bristol in a minute. I just wanted to come and see you before I left."

Stephanie closed her eyes, feeling stupid for thinking Meredith would be sticking around. She had already told her, in that hellhole, she wasn't from here. What an idiot to even think someone like her would even want to remain in a place where she had nearly died.

"It's okay, Mare. I don't know why I even asked."

"Hey, look at me." Stephanie shifted her gaze to capture hers. "It's not stupid to need someone. We went through hell in there and it's going to be hard to adjust to normality."

Stephanie didn't know what to say. Panic coursed through her again at the realisation that when she got out of the hospital, she would be alone. She had no one. Except for Joe, but he was married and had the gallery to run. He wouldn't have time to babysit her.

"What's wrong? Steph?"

She shook her head, fighting hard not to let the tears escape her eyes. "Nothing. I'm fine." Changing the subject, she asked, "Is Kathleen here?" As if conjured by her words, Kathleen appeared at the door.

"Oh, sweetheart, there you are," Kathleen said.

Stephanie caught her breath. The woman, who walked like she floated on air, came into her room and looked amazing. Not a hair out of place, trim and fit body, and curves in all the right places, wearing a suit which had to be tailor-made for her. She glided over to Meredith and possessively put a hand on her shoulder and bent down to kiss her cheek. Stephanie could swear she saw Meredith flinch at the contact.

"I'm sorry, Kath. I was just saying goodbye." Meredith's eyes held Stephanie's, regret clearly in them. "Stephanie Edwards, this is my partner, Kathleen Bowden-Scott. Kathleen, this is Stephanie."

Kathleen's gaze drifted briefly over Stephanie before settling back on Meredith. Stephanie felt the dismissal like a punch in the gut. She always knew she never did measure up with the elite in life, but it had never bothered her more than now, in Meredith's presence.

"The car is waiting," Kathleen said, as though introductions hadn't just been made. "Carrie-Ann is at your place now, making it comfortable for you. You've been gone so long." A small sob escaped her throat and Stephanie rolled her eyes at Kathleen's overly dramatic actions.

"I'm looking forward to seeing Carrie. I've missed her and Holly." Meredith turned to Stephanie. "I'm not sure if I mentioned Carrie to you, she is one of my closest friends. She just got married."

"Cool," Stephanie said.

A thick tension filled the room, and no one spoke for a few moments. Meredith turned to Kathleen.

"Can you give us a minute? I'll be out in second." Without giving Kathleen time to respond, she turned back to Stephanie.

Kathleen huffed and left the room.

Meredith placed her hand onto Stephanie's shoulder once the door shut behind Kathleen.

"That probably sounded a bit rude, but she's been a little overbearing since she arrived three days ago."

"Do you know how long I was there?"

"About a month. We were both lucky to survive. You nearly didn't." She sniffed and wiped at the moisture gathering in the corner of her eyes. "Look, I have to go. I need to get home, but I can't go not knowing if you're going to be all right."

"I'll be fine. Once I get out of here." Her smile was fake, and she could see in Meredith's eyes that she knew it too.

Meredith rose stiffly out of the wheelchair and pulled open a drawer in the bedside cabinet. Not finding what she was looking for, she opened another one. A victory smiled stretched across her lips. Leaning onto the top of the cabinet she wrote for a few seconds. Straightening up she turned to Stephanie.

"I've written down my email and home number. Call me or write me whenever, if you need anything."

Stephanie smiled gratefully. Her own eyes misted over now.

"Thank you."

Meredith leaned over and embraced her hard. Whispering into Stephanie's ear, she said, "Look after yourself. I'm glad you're safe." Before Stephanie could say anything, Meredith sat back in the wheelchair, grabbed the wheels, and rolled out of the room. Not glancing back once.

Stephanie took a deep breath, and after a minute of silence, her hand came to her mouth as sobs tore from her throat. It's a fine time to start feeling things. I'm truly alone!

CHAPTER FIVE

"It's been a really long drive. I just want to sleep."

After being in a car for nearly six hours, listening to Kathleen chat about all that had happened whilst she was "away," as she called it, Meredith just wanted to lie in her own bed and sleep for as long as possible. Her anxiety at being out in the open worried her. She hadn't told Kathleen, but being outside, seeing people, terrified her. Her heart pounded against her rib cage, her pulse missing the occasional beat. She needed peace. She needed the safety of her home. Even the spring flowers lining the roadway didn't hold the beauty they once did for her. She used to love springtime. To her it was the start of new life and growth, and she loved going for morning walks in the emerging sunlight, enjoying the longer days. Not anymore. Now, everything looked plain and gloomy. She just wanted to be home.

"Oh, okay," Kathleen said. "Um…I think Carrie will be there. Do you want me to call ahead and tell her to go?"

"No, it's all right. I won't mind seeing her for a few minutes." She turned her head, resting it on the window, and closed her eyes. Being out was nothing like she had imagined. She assumed she would feel relief at being home, getting back to normal. But she had been out for nearly a week and she still felt trapped in that hovel. Her life was gone, and she had no idea how to get it back.

They arrived at Meredith's apartment block a little before five that evening. The air inside the car felt too oppressive, so Meredith yanked the door open, escaping into the cool fresh air. She breathed in deeply, a small smile tugging at her lips at the sight of her home.

She lived in a purpose-built building that held only four apartments, one on each floor. Her apartment on the top floor was substantial, with three bedrooms and two baths. She thanked her lucky stars that she worked as an estate agent and had managed to secure this place at such a great deal. She owned it free and clear, thanks to an inheritance from her great-grandmother's passing.

Kathleen came around the front of the car and reached a hand out toward her. Meredith's eyes grew wide. She hastily shoved her hands into the pockets of her jeans and strode up the narrow walk to the main door. If Kathleen noticed the brush off, she didn't show it.

The sense of safety Meredith felt as soon as she entered her open-planned apartment gripped her forcibly. She hadn't felt this safe since she was driving in her car on the way to the meeting the day she was kidnapped. She quickly took in all the details of her home. To her left was the kitchen, up ahead was a corridor leading to the bedrooms and bathrooms, and to the right was the living room, complete with a three-seater contemporary sofa, fireplace, and a large widescreen TV. Her gaze scanned the lounge. Sitting in an oversized armchair by the big bay windows was her best friend Carrie. Her hand went to her mouth and a small sob escaped.

"Oh Jesus, Meredith! It's been so long," Carrie said.

Meredith took a few steps toward Carrie, Carrie did the same, but before she could reach her Meredith stopped. She really wanted to hug her, the need within her was great, but the thought of having someone touch her rattled her. Carrie seemed to sense her hesitancy and settled for just touching her shoulder lightly. Meredith was grateful. She didn't want to have to explain how she was feeling when she could hardly understand it herself.

"It's so good to see you, Carrie." She impatiently swiped at the tears on her cheeks as she sat on the grey leather sofa. Thoughts were swirling around her mind maddeningly. It felt surreal to be back home with her friend, in safety.

"Honey? Can I get you a drink?" Kathleen asked.

"No, that's okay, I'm fine. But thanks anyway."

Kathleen didn't seem to take any notice, going into the kitchen to put the kettle on. Meredith caught Carrie's confused look at Kathleen pottering around in the kitchen with jerky, hesitant movements.

"Is she okay?"

"I'm not sure. It's obviously been hard for her since I've been gone. I don't think she is taking this very well."

Carrie eyed her sympathetically.

"I can't imagine what it has been like for all of you, I'm just glad to be home," Meredith continued.

"Yes, we all kind of assumed you were dead. You were gone for so long that we didn't know what to do. Kathleen had all but shut down your home. When I heard you were rescued, I had your utilities switched back on and I restocked your cupboards and fridge today."

"Thank you for that. And it really is great to see you."

"I know it's going to be hard for you, being back here and adjusting to a normal life again, but your family and friends are here to support you."

Meredith smiled at her friend. They had met nearly a year ago through a mutual acquaintance, and Carrie had contacted her when she needed to find a new apartment and a residency for her new business. They had become firm friends and Meredith was glad she had her in her life. She could hear Kathleen making the tea in the kitchen and wondered again how she was coping with all of this. Kathleen hadn't spoken much about her disappearance while she was in the hospital. She had just flitted about, making sure Meredith was comfortable and had everything she needed. She was glad of the help and attention, but it was starting to smother her. She doubted Kathleen would understand she didn't want to be touched. She would only take it as a rejection and Meredith couldn't be dealing with her dramas.

"I'm not sure what to say to you, Meredith," Carrie said, breaking her musings. "I want to ask about what happened, but I can only assume that it was horrific and it's not something you particularly want to talk about."

"Well, yes, it wasn't the best vacation I've ever taken, hospitality was shocking." Meredith knew her tone was angry and being sarcastic was the only way she could deal with her emotions now. "I'm definitely not the same woman I was before I was taken. I have some hideous scars."

The tea tray Kathleen carried over to the coffee table at that moment clattered loudly in her hands as she approached.

"And they will probably take some healing," Meredith finished.

Kathleen set the tray down, took her mobile phone out of her pocket, and excused herself to the spare bedroom to make a call. Meredith knew she couldn't get away quick enough from the talk of the horrendous things she had been through.

"Well, that was rude," Carrie said.

"I can't blame her. I'm not the looker I once was. Kathleen has always been attracted to beautiful things, and I was one of her possessions. I'm not saying she is shallow, but the way I look now, that would be hard for anybody to look at."

"God's sake, Meredith! You've been through hell. You're lucky to even be here. If she loves you it shouldn't matter what you look like."

"I know, but that isn't how life works in her circles. I don't blame her, I can barely tolerate looking at myself in the mirror. I will always have scars, on the inside and out, and I'm okay with that, I think."

Meredith set about pouring tea for them all, smiling to herself. Kathleen did know her, at least a little bit. She knew even though Meredith said she didn't want tea Kathleen recognised she was parched and a refreshing cuppa was just what she needed. She hoped, with time, perhaps Kathleen could learn to accept the way she looked now. Her face had one small scar across her cheek, about an inch long, but barely noticeable. It was her torso and breasts that were the worst. To look at Meredith's face you wouldn't even know she had spent eight months being brutally victimised. If she ever could find it in herself to make love again, she would make sure the lights were off and Kathleen wouldn't be able to see her body.

"I have been through a lot, but I'm glad Stephanie was there." At Carrie's raised eyebrows she continued. "She was a woman who was there with me, she was there about a month in the end. He had plenty more women there as well, so I'm assuming he ran out of space to put us all in. We ended up being in the same room for all that time, talking, comforting, and praying together that we wouldn't die. I hope she's okay."

"She must have been through hell as well. It must have been scary not knowing what was going to happen."

Meredith ran her hand through her hair, letting out a deep breath. She could feel her heart rate pick up again as the anxiety of being back in that room filled her. She briefly closed her eyes, concentrating on the image of Stephanie in the hospital bed, eyes open, a smile on her face. Thinking back to earlier that morning she had no choice but to see Stephanie before she left. There was no way she could leave Yorkshire without at least making sure Stephanie was going to get better. She knew they had bonded in that hellhole and she hoped she would be in contact.

"It's definitely something neither one of us would ever want to experience again, but I think we were both glad we had someone we could talk to."

Carrie glanced at the clock mounted over the fireplace, and then back at Meredith. She was about to speak when Kathleen came out of the bedroom, putting her phone in her pocket.

"I'm going to head home, love. There is a problem at the office and I need to take a conference call with some of the other partners." She didn't give Meredith a chance to respond. She grabbed her handbag off the kitchen island and strode purposefully toward her. It looked to Meredith as if she wanted to kiss her goodbye, but Kathleen stopped herself at the last second. She hesitated and grimaced.

"I'll be at the office tomorrow and I'll probably stay over in London for the night as I have business meetings the next day. I'll call you when I can." Then she left, not giving Meredith a chance to even say goodbye.

Meredith turned around and fiddled with her cup, swirling the tea. She regarded Carrie, whose mouth was hanging open in shock.

"Carrie, honestly, it's fine. We have been together for a long time, but for a lot of that time we worked in different parts of the country. It's not unusual for her to be gone for days at a time."

"Yes, but you have just got back from a fucking kidnapping! How in the hell can she leave you with everything that you've been through?"

Meredith shook her head. "I'm actually glad she's not going to be here. I know that sounds bad, but all I want to do is put on my pyjamas, curl up in bed, and sleep for as long as possible. I don't think I could handle her fussing around me anyway."

"I know that's what you're saying, but are you sure you're going to be okay on your own? I can always call Holly and stay here with you if you want."

"I'm sure. I'll be fine. I really do just want to have some time by myself. Catch up on a few things and speak to my family. I spoke to my mum at the hospital and she and dad are flying back from New York at the end of the week. It'll give me some time to prepare for their visit."

Carrie rose from the chair and took the tea tray to the kitchen. After swilling everything out and leaving the cups to drain, she came back to Meredith who was standing, leaning back on the arm of the sofa. Meredith could see the concern in her eyes.

"I promise I'm fine."

Carrie came to stand directly in front of her and Meredith could see the tears gathering. She didn't think, she gathered Carrie into her arms and held her tightly. Panic set in, she swore her heart was going to beat right out of her chest. Anxiety gripped her hard, her body vibrating with fear. As if sensing her discomfort, Carrie disentangled herself from her and stepped back, wiping her eyes as she did so.

"I'm sorry, I can tell physical contact is hard for you now."

"You needed that hug just as much as I did. I need to start getting back to normal. Shying away from contact isn't going to solve anything. And besides, I wanted to hug you the second I saw you."

They said their goodbyes at the door and Meredith turned to face her home. For the first time in days, weeks really, she was alone. Without giving it much thought, she grabbed her laptop off her small desk in the corner of the lounge and headed straight to her bedroom. Once inside her room, she stripped off, then put on her most comfortable, softest pyjamas. She climbed into bed, settling her laptop on her lap. She switched it on, glad it still held a charge after all this time and spent the next couple of hours going through her emails and trying to sort out some semblance of order in all she had missed in the last eight-and-a-half months.

Finally, sometime later, her eyes closed, and she began to drift off to sleep, Stephanie's smiling face filling her mind's eye.

CHAPTER SIX

Stephanie walked through the front door of the Genesis Gallery in York. She cast her gaze around the small lobby, taking in all the originals and prints of local artists in one sweep, finally settling on the man behind a contemporary steel desk. Joseph Mathews had owned this gallery for the last five years after buying it from his father. She had come to him three years ago, having just completed her master's degree in fine art, looking for a job. He had been so impressed with her and her portfolio that he hired her on the spot, and over the next six months trained her up to help run his business.

"Bloody hell, Steph, you look like shit!" He came around the desk and engulfed her in a tight, bear hug, squeezing her into his muscled chest. She flinched at the contact, but soon the familiar strength of him settled her racing pulse. Her arms came around his waist as she buried her face into his neck inhaling his expensive aftershave. He was a big man, just topping six feet, and his body showed off the years spent in the gym working on his muscles. He filled out his jeans and white shirt to perfection. Looking at him always made Stephanie want to take her own physical shape seriously, but she just couldn't envision herself spending all those hours lifting weights and doing cardio. She preferred pizza and beer.

"Hey, Joe." She took another deep breath and gently pulled back. She had to tilt her head to look him in the eye. "I'm hoping I still have a job and a home."

She lived in the apartment above the gallery. It wasn't the largest of spaces, having been converted from the loft, but it was big enough for her and her needs.

"Don't be stupid, Squirt, you know you'll always have a place with me." Joe went to the front door, flipped the sign closed, and locked the door. He took her hand and led her to the back room. They settled onto a ratty three-seater sofa facing each other.

"I was shocked to get your call. You'd been gone for a month and every time I called the police for an update, they basically told me not to keep my hopes up. Couldn't believe it when you rang, I very nearly pissed my pants when I heard your voice. I would have come down to see you, you know?"

"I know, but there really wasn't any point. I was just lying in a hospital bed. There was nothing you could have done." The thought of Joe seeing just how bad she was when she was rescued terrified her. She wouldn't have been able to deal with his sympathies. She needed time to heal without feeling like a victim.

"I could have been there for you." He lifted his hand and gently touched her right eyebrow, tracing the healing scar with his finger. "I assume they caught that fucker."

"Yeah, he tried to take somebody else but failed, and from her description they managed to catch him. Eventually they found us." Her mind travelled to Meredith, and she wondered how she was doing. Stephanie had got out of the hospital that morning, which was four days after Meredith had left. Stephanie hadn't been able to get her out of her mind. She hoped Meredith was okay, that she was dealing with everything all right, and that Kathleen was taking care of her. "The prick had taken quite a few of us, some of us didn't make it. I have to go to the station in a couple of days to make a statement."

Joe took her hand in his larger one and gently kissed her knuckles.

"If you want, you can come and stay with me and Fiona, we would love to have you."

"Thanks for the offer, but I would just rather get back to my normal routine. If you give me the rest of the week off for my bruises to fade and talk to the police, I can start back again on Monday."

She could feel Joe's eyes studying her, what he was trying to see she didn't know. She was aware of the purple and yellow bruises that covered her face and neck, but with a good base of make-up she should be able to hide them. She hoped Joe was looking at the bruises and not trying to see something within her that just wasn't there. She never really had any kind of feelings before, as she told Meredith, she was merely content in her life. After what happened to her, she doubted that would ever change, and if Joe hoped to see some sort of emotion regarding her time in captivity, he wouldn't find any. She was angry, thoroughly pissed off that the prick had dared to touch her; she hated the things he had done to Meredith, but she wasn't going to wallow in self-pity. She wanted to get her life back to the way it was. Doing her routine things, going about her routine life, was the only way she was going to cope with this.

After what felt like years of Joe peering into her soul, he finally spoke. "Are you sure about coming back to work so soon?"

"Yeah, I'll be fine."

Today was Wednesday; the police interview was on Friday, so they both agreed to start back to work on Monday would be the best thing to do.

"Everything is as you left it upstairs. I've put one of the company mobile phones up there for you to use, and some essentials. Go on up and get settled and I'll call for a pizza delivery."

She started to protest, but he pushed her toward the stairs that led up through the back of the building into her apartment, following close behind. He didn't give her a chance to argue. She might like to do things on her own, and without help, but apparently, he would be damned if she couldn't at least share a pizza with him.

"The pizza should be here in twenty minutes," Joe said, putting his phone back in his pocket as he turned away from the living room window that overlooked the street below. She could feel his gaze on her and she struggled not to squirm under his watchful eyes.

"Joe, can you stop looking at me like that? I don't know what it is you're looking for, but it's not in there."

He walked over to where she stood in the small kitchen, her hands braced behind her on the kitchen sink.

"Not being funny, Squirt, but you have been through hell..."

"Do you still have to call me that? I'm five feet eight inches, which is hardly short."

"You'll always be Squirt to me. As I was saying, you've been through God knows what, and you're standing here as if nothing happened. When you called me from the hospital you didn't sound upset at all. You practically sounded like you had just come back from holiday."

"Come on, Joe, I wasn't that bad. You know what I'm like." She charged past him, nudging him out of the way as she went. She stood where he stood five minutes ago and stared at the street below. She could see people bustling about, going on about their daily business, and she just wanted to be one of them again. She wanted to forget everything that had happened. "I've had shit happen to me before, don't forget."

"I'm not talking about your mother dying in a car accident when you were a baby, or your useless father walking out on you. You were kidnapped, tortured, and God knows what else. There's got to be something you're feeling about this." He came up behind her and put his hands on her shoulders, squeezing gently.

She wasn't expecting his hands to be placed on her and she thought she might flinch at the contact, but she didn't, she didn't feel anything. She turned around, her eyes pleading with Joe to understand.

"I don't know what's wrong with me. The only time I felt anything was when he was hurting Meredith." At his questioning look, she continued. "She had been there several months before I even arrived, and he did terrible things to her. The only time I cried was when she was in pain. I didn't

42

cry for me, I was angry at him for what he was doing, but I stuck it in the back of my mind and just ignored it the best I could."

He pulled her into him again.

"I love you, Squirt. Don't forget that." He released her from his hug as she sat down on the small coffee table. "Do you think you should try counselling again?"

"I don't think so. It didn't work the first time, they didn't find anything wrong with me. I just don't feel things the way other people do. I can empathise with others, but for some reason I can't feel anything for me. I guess I think I'm just not worth it."

"Now you know that's a load of bullocks. You're a great person, Steph, and one of these days, you will realise that you're worth loving."

Stephanie looked at him as if he had grown two heads. No one stuck around for her, she was a cancer on people's lives and nothing anyone said was ever going to change that. The sooner she went about her business the better.

†

Meredith woke to the sound of her landline ringing. She stretched and yawned and absently glanced at the clock, noting the time was eight-thirty in the morning. She had been home now for five days and she had left the apartment only once. Kathleen had been by a couple of times but never stayed for too long. Meredith could understand her feelings, it was hard to deal with a victim of trauma. Kathleen was doing everything right, she brought food, she helped do the cooking and cleaning, and she made mindless small talk. Meredith felt like a heel. Kathleen was being attentive, but she obviously picked up on her need to be alone. Kathleen never pressed her to talk about what happened during the months she had been gone. It was almost like she was trying to forget it ever happened. Meredith was fine with that, she hoped she could forget it as well.

She picked up the phone in the living room.

"Hello?"

"Hello. Is this Meredith Ashcroft?"

"Yes, speaking."

"I'm calling from the city police station. We need you to come to the station to make a formal statement and go over a few things. Today, if it's convenient."

"I'm sorry, but that won't be possible. There is no way I'm leaving my apartment. If you want to talk to me then you will have to come here." She was being short, she knew, but she didn't care. Just the thought of leaving her home brought her out in a cold sweat.

"Miss Ashcroft, there are some things we need you to look at and go through. It would be best if you could make it to the station."

"Look, officer, I'm not going anywhere. As I'm sure you can imagine, I've had a pretty shitty time and nothing and no one is making me leave my apartment until I'm ready."

The officer must have realised his mistake because he acquiesced to Meredith's wishes.

"Okay. I'll send a detective to see you this afternoon."

They arranged a time, and Meredith hung up, blowing out a deep breath. The last thing she wanted to do was talk about her time in that hellhole. She had no choice if she wanted that asshole put away. She would have to do everything in her power to make that so. She picked up the receiver again and dialled Kathleen's number.

Kathleen answered on the third ring, her voice sounding tired. "Meredith? Are you okay?"

"I know it's early, Kath, but I just had a call from the police station. They are coming here this afternoon to take my statement. I was hoping you could be here with me."

"Peaches, I would love to be there to help you, but I have a meeting with a client in Reading. I don't think I'll be back in time."

Meredith wondered idly if this was Kathleen's attempt to distance herself from the horrible things Meredith had been through. She knew Kathleen could be somewhat superficial, but she prayed her distance wasn't because of the way she looked now. Taking a gamble, she asked, "Are you okay, Kath? Is there anything we need to talk about?"

"I'm not sure what you mean, babe. If I didn't have client meetings, of course, I would be there for you." She took a breath, then continued. "I think maybe we need to take some time out. It's not what you're thinking. It's just with the new season coming, I have a lot of clients that need my attention and I don't feel I can be there for you the way you need. You know I love you, sweetie, but I'm thinking about what is best for you. I think it would best if you took some time to heal and then call me."

Is she fucking kidding me? Meredith tried to understand what Kathleen was saying. She knew they had been plodding along in their relationship, it was somewhat pleasant at times, and she didn't believe for a second, they were destined to be life partners. But she couldn't believe Kathleen would be so cold and just turn her back on her.

"I know I have a few scars, and my head is a bit messed up right now, but surely you're not that shallow that my looks are all you care about?"

45

"You've got it wrong, Meredith, I do love you, you know that, but I'm not sure I'm strong enough to handle this. I don't know what it is you need. I don't know what else I can give you."

"I'm not asking you to do anything Kathleen, just be there for me, if you can."

Meredith knew she was being clingy, but she only had a few people in her world that she trusted. Excluding family, Carrie was one, and Kathleen was the other. Her parents would be arriving in a few days and she wanted to have some semblance of her life back in order before they arrived. She did not want her mother hovering around her. Her mother would be there for her, without question, but there were some things she didn't need her mother to know, and the horror she experienced in that place was one of them.

She loved Kathleen, she might not be in love with her the way she once was when they first started dating, but she still loved her, and she needed her. In what capacity that was she didn't know yet.

"I'm not saying I'm ready to have a physical relationship with you, because let's face it, I'm not, but I need you here as my friend. I think after all the years we've been together, that's the least we can do for each other."

"You're right. I just feel shitty for not knowing what it is you need, I feel helpless. I'll call my client and rearrange the meeting. I'm still in Bristol so I will be there when the police come."

Meredith let out the breath she didn't know she was holding, relief washing through her. Yes, they had their share of relationship problems, but they did love each other, and Meredith needed her.

"Thank you, you have no idea what that means to me. I'm sorry for making this difficult for you, but the things I went through..."

"So, I'll see you at lunchtime."

Meredith blinked at the interruption. She was right, Kathleen obviously didn't want to know what she had been through, but at some point, they were going to have to talk about it.

"Um, the officers will be here at one-thirty, I'll see you then." They said their goodbyes and she hung up.

Glancing at the clock that sat on the mantelpiece, she noted it was nine-thirty. She decided to go back to bed. Her body clock was still all over the place, and she felt eternally tired from her ordeal. She needed the rest. Well, that's what she told herself, she just didn't want to face the world. She climbed into her bed, set the alarm clock, closed her eyes, and pretended she wasn't anxious about the meeting this afternoon.

CHAPTER SEVEN

Meredith sat at her oak dining table, located in the corner of the expansive kitchen. She had a hot cup of coffee cradled in her left hand, and in her right, she held tightly to Kathleen's hand. To Kathleen's credit, she showed up early and had set about trying to make Meredith feel as comfortable as possible about the upcoming interview. She had been courteous and gracious to the female detective who sat opposite them now.

The officer was maybe one inch shorter than Meredith's own five feet six. She wore a casual grey suit with a white shirt, and her hair fell loosely about her face to her shoulders. She had introduced herself as Detective Constable Walker and she had been assigned to the case in conjunction with the officers in York.

"Let me just start by saying I know how difficult this must be for you, Meredith," the officer said.

Meredith spared a quick glance at Kathleen. She was staring down at the table, and by the look on her face, trying to distance herself as much as possible from the conversation. Looking back into the detective's sympathetic brown eyes, Meredith said, "I'm not particularly handling this very well. I have spoken to my doctor and she is recommending a counsellor for me, one who can deal with these types of situations."

"That's good. I'm hoping with your statement, and that of the other survivors, it'll help put him behind bars. I don't know if you are aware that he is denying the charges against him, he said he hadn't been to that house in years."

"How can he say that?" Meredith gasped. "You have a witness that identified him trying to kidnap her. It's ridiculous."

"It's okay, Meredith. We have a lot of evidence against him, including all the physical evidence we collected in the house. I promise you he won't get away with this."

The detective took a sip of her coffee and opened her notepad. She placed a small tape recorder in the middle of the table.

"Is it okay if I record this?"

"Of course."

"I think it's best if you just recount the events to the best of your knowledge and at the end of your statement, I'll ask any questions I feel are pertinent to the case. Is that all right?"

"Yes, that's fine." She thought for a few moments, trying to organise the events in her mind, and hoping when she spoke of what happened, her voice wouldn't tremble, and she wouldn't break down. "I'm not really sure how much I can tell you, I didn't really see his face. Every time he did anything to me, he wore a baseball cap pulled low over his forehead and a bandanna wrapped around his nose and mouth. I could tell you what he smells like, being that close to him for long periods of time, it isn't a smell I will forget any time soon."

She spent the next two hours detailing everything she could remember about her time in captivity. Every time she got to a particularly harrowing part, she could feel Kathleen stiffen beside her. She could only imagine what it must be like for the lover of someone to listen to the things that had happened to them. She knew herself if it had been Kathleen who was captured, she doubted she would handle it very well at all. At one point during the interview, when she detailed the time he had cut her body hundreds of times, Kathleen excused herself to the bathroom. Meredith could hear retching sounds coming from behind the door.

"I'm sorry you had to go through all that again, Meredith, I can see it was hard for you," the officer said. They walked to the door, Officer Walker searching for her car keys in her bag. "I shall get this transcribed and sent off to the officers who are dealing with the case in York."

Meredith looked over at Kathleen, who was staring out of the lounge window, not paying them any mind, lost in her own thoughts. She looked back to the officer who was now standing over the threshold.

"I don't suppose you have heard anything from a woman called Stephanie Edwards?" At Officer Walker's questioning glance, she explained. "She was another victim who was in the same room as me."

"I'm sorry, no. I was just given the bare bone facts in your individual case to interview you with."

"That's okay, I just wondered."

They said their goodbyes and Meredith closed the door. Walking over to Kathleen she asked, "Are you okay?"

Kathleen shook her head and turned to face her. Meredith could see the anguish in her eyes. She had never seen so much torment in her before.

"How the hell did you survive that, Meredith?"

The absence of the pet names didn't escape her notice. Kathleen might not have been aware of it, but she was gradually distancing herself from Meredith.

"I probably would have died after a week."

"I can honestly say that I didn't choose to survive. It's not like I felt a powerful fight or flight in me. I just did as I was told and tried not to make him too angry. You don't know what you would do in those situations until they happen to you. I'm sure you could have survived it too."

"That's nice of you to say, but we both know I would have crumbled the second he got his hands on me."

Meredith was unsure what to say. It was true, Kathleen wasn't a very strong person. When it came to business Kathleen's mind was as sharp as a knife, and she had a penchant for pretty things. She was high society and nothing of the real world really touched her. She had a good heart and a brilliant mind, but she had built a wall around herself where no pain, or emotion could go. They rarely talked of anything significant and Meredith would be hard pressed to name even one memory from Kathleen's childhood. She was closed off and Meredith had found herself comparing Kathleen to Stephanie. Stephanie didn't have much to say about growing up when they had talked in-between visits from the Man. As far as Meredith could tell, Stephanie's childhood had been a disaster, something obviously had happened back then that still affected her. Meredith wondered why she was more concerned with how Stephanie was feeling right now instead of Kathleen.

†

It was Friday night and Meredith was alone. She hadn't heard from Kathleen since she left yesterday afternoon, not even a text message. She knew that Kathleen was struggling with the events that had taken place, so she was willing to give her some space, some time to process everything. Her parents would be arriving tomorrow, so she set about cleaning up one of the two spare bedrooms, putting fresh sheets on the bed, and puttering around. At nine o'clock she had finished all the chores she had wanted to get done and decided to have a glass of wine in bed while surfing the Internet.

After grabbing a bottle of Pinot Noir and a glass from the kitchen, she readied herself for bed. She got comfortable, had a sip of wine, and began surfing. She hadn't had a drink for months now and the earthy flavours warmed her insides. After browsing random websites and watching a few videos on YouTube, she opened her email. She wasn't expecting anything important since she was still on extended leave from her business. Her business partner had everything under control, just as he had in the past eight months. They had agreed that he would keep running things until Meredith felt ready to come back, whenever that would be.

Her eyes roamed over the few unimportant notifications until her gaze landed on an email address and subject line which made her heart flutter. It was from Stephanie, titled "how are things?" Her finger hovered over the touchpad, debating whether to open the email or not. Stephanie had been on her mind a lot since she left the hospital a week ago, and she was dismayed at the nervousness she felt coursing through her body. Deciding she was being stupid, she clicked open the email.

Hey, Meredith, I hope this reaches you. I'm not sure if you were serious about me keeping in contact but wanted to check in with you and see how you are. I went to the police station this morning and gave my statement. Don't know if you have spoken to them yet, but apparently Jameson West (that's the bastard's name) is denying everything. I guess I just wanted to connect with you, make sure you're okay, and that Kathleen is taking care of you.

Well, I guess that's it. I'm okay. I'm back at work on Monday, things are getting back to normal. Reply if you like. Or not, whatever you think is best. It would be nice to hear from you.

Best wishes, Steph.

Meredith read the email three more times trying to gauge the sense of Stephanie, and of how she was feeling. She said she was fine, but Meredith didn't believe that for a second. She had a big gulp of her wine and thought about her response because she was going to reply. There was no doubt about that. She clicked on the reply icon and began to type.

Hi Stephanie, it's good to hear from you! I had an officer come to my apartment yesterday afternoon and I gave my statement to her. It's good to hear that you're doing okay and, to be honest, I'm not faring so well. I'm struggling to even go outside of the apartment. My business partner has been amazing, keeping things going for me at work, but I'm not sure if I'll be up to going back there anytime soon.

I'm not sure what to say about Kathleen. She hasn't really been here since I've been home, but that's okay with me. I'm not sure what to say to her most of the time. I know she doesn't want to hear about the things that happened to me, I can't say I blame her. I shouldn't be so hard on her, she is doing everything that she can, that she knows how to, and it's hard for her. I'm not even sure why I'm telling you this. I guess it's easy to say how you are feeling when you are not facing someone in person.

I really hope that guy doesn't get away with this, he should be hanged! It's a shame we don't do that in this country anymore. Please do keep in contact, I feel strangely comforted knowing you are there, thinking of me.

Meredith.

She read over what she had written, making sure it sounded okay. She contemplated deleting the things about Kathleen, but decided it felt good to talk about it. She could talk to Carrie, but she knew what Carrie would say. She would tell her Kathleen was selfish and needed to get her head out of her ass. Stephanie didn't know Kathleen and somehow it felt safer. She took another sip of wine, to fortify herself, and then hit the send icon. Not wanting to wait up and see if Stephanie would respond, she closed the lid on her laptop, put it on the floor, and drained the rest of her wine. She went to the bathroom to brush her teeth and then went to bed, another night with Stephanie at the forefront of her mind.

CHAPTER EIGHT

Stephanie rolled over in bed. The muted noise of Joe opening the gallery below must have disturbed her in her sleep. She glanced at the clock, knowing if Joe was opening it was likely to be close to nine o'clock. She had gone to bed early last night; the constant checking of her email was driving her insane. She didn't know whether to expect a reply from Meredith, but she had hoped. Apart from Joe, Stephanie had not felt a connection to another human being in her life. Something about Meredith seemed to draw her in. She wasn't stupid, she knew that being together in that room probably caused some sort of emotional connection. But she couldn't deny the sense of safety she had felt holding Meredith's hand, looking at her beautiful face, and holding her close. The attachment she felt might not be realistic, but she didn't care. For the first time in her life she felt something for someone.

She got out of bed and went into the kitchen and fixed herself a bowl of cereal. As she sat down at the small dinette table, she grabbed her phone and opened her email application. Her breath caught as she spied the reply from Meredith. Quickly she opened it. As she read the words, she couldn't stop a small tear from escaping down her cheek. She had thought Meredith and Kathleen were a stable couple. It was true that Meredith never really spoke of her whilst they were in captivity, but she just assumed it was the shock and fear of being where they were. Stephanie hated the thought of her being alone in her apartment with no one to comfort her. She hoped her friend Carrie was at least being somewhat helpful.

Stephanie failed to recognise the parallel with her own life. She too was sitting in her apartment on her own with no one for comfort, and that was fine with her. Stephanie was great, she didn't need anybody. She had Joe and even he could be somewhat over the top for her liking. She was glad Meredith's parents were arriving this weekend. She didn't know a lot about them, but if Meredith was an example of their parentage, they were good people.

Stephanie opened the reply box and began to type.

Meredith, I'm disheartened to hear that you are feeling so low at the minute. I had wished you might be getting back on track with the help of Kathleen and your friends. I'm glad your parents are arriving this weekend; hopefully, they will be able to help you. Don't forget I am always here if you need me. It feels good to be connected to you too. Let me know how things go with your parents, and I'll update you if I hear anything from the police.

Enjoy your weekend, email me anytime.

Stephanie.

She sent the email on its way and finished eating her breakfast. She had no plans for the day and decided that going down to help Joe would be just what she needed to take her mind off things. They had agreed she wouldn't be back until Monday but sitting in this apartment was going to drive her crazy. She had never been one to sit and do nothing, always finding things to occupy her time. She would put some make-up on the bruises to cover them up as best she could, and hope Joe wouldn't mind the help.

†

Meredith had received a text message from Kathleen just after dawn, simply stating she would pick up Meredith's parents from the airport for her. She was shocked at the abrupt tone. It wasn't like Kathleen not to have a pet name in there for her and to end the text message with a couple of kisses. The absence of both confirmed that things were taking a different route for them. The growing distance between them was getting wider by the day. At least they were still friends, for now. They might not have admitted it to each other, but she knew their relationship was over. She couldn't be what Kathleen needed and Kathleen clearly couldn't be someone Meredith needed now. She replied to the text message with a simple okay and thank you. She spent the next hour in bed procrastinating about ending their relationship and wondering if she wanted to change the way things were going. She didn't.

A couple of hours later Meredith was sitting at the dining room table with her laptop open, reading Stephanie's latest message. It was nice to have her support and understanding. After all, Stephanie had been there with her through the ordeal and it had bonded them together. She was about to reply when the front door opened, and Kathleen came through, Meredith's parents trailing behind. Before she had a chance to even think, her mother engulfed her in a tight hug. Her mother was the same height as Meredith and the same curly red hair was now greying at the temples.

"Oh, my dearest Meredith, I'm so glad you are okay."

"Good to see you, Mum."

She pulled back slightly and looked over her mother's shoulder. Her dad still stood in the entryway. He looks scared, unsure of what to do. He was standing stiffly, looking everywhere except at Meredith, his luggage still held firmly in his hands. She dropped her arms from her mother's waist and went to her father. She took the luggage from him, placing it on the floor, and then gently, fighting her new tendency to resist bodily contact, put her arms around him. She sensed his struggle with his emotions.

"Hey, Dad."

His face crumpled and racking great sobs left his body.

"My baby girl!"

She held him tight. She didn't know what to say. Her dad had always been the strong one, the one to make everyone feel better. Now the roles were reversed, and she found herself comforting him. She didn't mind, though, and it made a change from the self-pity she was feeling most of the time.

After a few moments of father and daughter comforting each other, Kathleen cleared her throat.

"I'll take the luggage into the spare room." Meredith watched her go with a thin smile on her lips. They were heading for a breakup, she could feel it.

She led her father over to the couch and sat with him while her mother went to make tea. Her mother always liked to be practical in any given situation, she never wallowed, always preferring to be moving around.

Kathleen emerged from the bedroom never once looking at Meredith, joining Meredith's mother in the kitchen. Meredith looked back to her father, who was wiping his eyes with a handkerchief. He smiled at her, a mixture of self-deprecation and embarrassment.

"Sorry about that, Mare. It's just I'm so glad to have you home. When you first went missing, your mum and I came home, but after three months the police told us not to keep our hopes up and try to go on about our lives." He took her hand and placed it on his cheek, holding it there. "I knew we should have stayed, tried harder to find you, but with the business…"

"It's okay, Dad. It took the police months to find us all."

Her mother placed the tea tray on the coffee table and joined her husband on the couch. She put her hand on his thigh and Meredith's heart warmed at the affection her parents still had for each other, even after thirty-nine years of marriage.

"I'm glad you didn't sit around awaiting news. I'm sure that would have driven you both crazy."

"Meredith?" Kathleen said as she came in from the kitchen. At Meredith's raised eyebrows, she said, "Can I have a quick word?"

Meredith excused herself from her parents and followed Kathleen back into the kitchen. She regarded Kathleen steadily. She looked terrible. There were dark circles under her eyes and her normally clear completion looked sallow.

"Kath?"

Kathleen folded her arms, resting them across her breasts, a classic defensive pose.

"I need to go to London for a few days. I have a client who is being particularly clingy, and he needs to see me."

Meredith tried to capture her gaze, but she kept them downcast.

She's lying.

"Are you sure everything is okay? I know you said the other day maybe we should take a break."

"No, everything is fine, I promise. This is a business. I'll call you when I arrive."

She didn't have a chance to reply. Kathleen brushed past her, said a quick goodbye to Meredith's parents, and was gone. Meredith slumped back against the counter.

Her mother came in and asked, "Who lit a fire under her ass?"

"Kath needs to go to London for work."

"But you've just got out of the hospital. Surely she should be taking care of you?"

"I think we might be breaking up." Meredith shook her head. She smiled tremulously and headed back into the lounge. "Did you save me any tea, Dad?"

Meredith could feel her mother's gaze on her as she walked away, but she refused to look back. Things with Kathleen were beyond repair and she found she didn't really mind. She needed to concentrate on getting better, on getting her strength back. She didn't have time for looking after other people, and until Kathleen decided she wanted to talk, they would just have to keep their distance from each other.

†

"Hey, Joe. How's business going today?"

Joe stood behind the counter wrapping a small watercolour print in bubble wrap for a customer. He glanced at her quickly before ringing up the purchase. The customer paid, and once he left, Joe turned fully to face Stephanie.

"I thought we agreed you weren't coming back until Monday. Good job on the make-up, though. Are you sure you want to be here?"

Stephanie blew out a breath, raking her fingers through her hair, and held Joe's gaze.

"You know me, Joe, I like to keep busy. I'm just sitting upstairs, surfing the net, and watching crap on the telly. I want to help."

"Well, it's pretty quiet now, I don't really need any help in the shop, but if you're desperate you could do me a favour and go through last month's receipts. I haven't really kept up with them since you've been away. I was never very good at it." He grinned. "I guess I must have always known you would be coming back. I saved them just for you."

Stephanie smiled back, glad that she had someone in her life who made her feel almost normal. She went to the small office out back and sat at Joe's desk. She began the laborious task of sorting through the last five weeks' worth of invoices, receipts, and bills.

A few hours later she heard the beep of an incoming email on her phone. She didn't pretend she wasn't waiting for one. Helping Joe was the only way she could distract her mind from thinking about Meredith. She grabbed her phone out of the pocket of her jeans and opened the email.

Hey, Steph. I hope everything is okay with you today and thank you for your support. My parents arrived this morning from New York, it was amazing to see them again. My mum was her usual self, taking care of the practical things like cleaning and making tea. It felt nice to have some sort of normality back. My dad was a little upset, well, devastated, to finally see me. He took my disappearance hard. I think the emotions of finally seeing me again were too much for him. It felt strange to hold him as he cried.

Carrie is coming over tonight and my mum is going to cook us all a meal. It'll be nice to have some home-cooked food; my mum's chilli is to die for.

How is your Saturday going?

Speak soon, Meredith.

As she finished reading the email, she wondered why Meredith hadn't mentioned Kathleen. She knew they were having some adjustment problems, but she hoped they were working on it. Meredith had been through such horrendous, evil things, she deserved to be looked after properly.

She was about to reply when Joe called to her from the front of the shop.

"Hey, Steph? Can you cover out here while I help carry this canvas to a customer's car?"

"Yeah, sure." She slipped her phone back into her pocket and went to do Joe's bidding, all the while thinking about what her reply would be to Meredith's email.

CHAPTER NINE

"Meredith, honey? I need to go get some ingredients for the meal tonight. Go pop your coat on and we can get going." Her mother didn't see the look of horror that passed across Meredith's face.

Just the mention of going outside filled her with dread. She still hadn't told her parents about her lack of ability to leave the apartment. She stood from her kitchen table, pushing the lid closed on her laptop as she went. Without giving it a thought, she went to the hall closet and popped on her parka coat. Her hands shook as she zipped it up and she could feel a light sheen of sweat forming on her forehead. Her breath came in quick gasps and black spots danced before her eyes. She was going down, she had never had a panic attack before, so she didn't know the symptoms, but surely this was it?

As she leaned back against the wall her mother came around the corner. Taking in Meredith's state she rushed to her daughter's side. She placed a hand on her shoulder and said, "Bloody hell, Meredith! Quick, sit down before you fall down."

Meredith slumped to the floor, pulling her knees up to her chest, resting her forehead on them. Her mother crouched down beside her and began rubbing soothing circles on her back.

She tried to control her breathing, but every breath caught in her throat. She was gripped by a full-blown panic attack.

"Harold?" Janet called.

Meredith's dad came into the hallway and took in the scene.

"Meredith? Baby, look at me."

In the back of her mind she thought it funny that her dad still called her "baby" even in her early forties. She lifted her head and gazed steadily into her father's eyes. She felt the strength in them, helping to ground her.

"Meredith, you need to slow down your breathing. Try to take a deep breath and let it out slowly."

She began breathing in time to her father's breaths, concentrating on holding his gaze with her own and the cadence he set. After a few moments her breathing settled, her head cleared.

"Thanks, Dad. I'm not sure what happened." She could see the look that passed between her parents, they didn't believe her, they damn well knew she was hiding something.

She stood and headed back to the lounge, discarding her coat on the back of the chair as she went. Her parents came in behind her and both took a seat facing her. They looked at her with sympathy and she found she could no longer hide what she was feeling.

"There's something I need to tell you both. I haven't been out of the house since I have been home. I don't know if it's some kind of PTSD, but I'm scared to go out the front door."

"Oh, sweetheart, why didn't you say anything?" Janet asked.

Meredith shrugged, not sure how to answer the question.

"I guess I didn't want to admit I was more affected by what happened than what I am. There's more." She waited for her parents to both look her in the eye and she said the hardest part. "I seem to have a problem with touch. If anybody touches me, I get filled with panic and I flinch."

"But we've been touching you since we've been here this morning," her father said. "In fact, you hugged me."

She could see the confusion on their faces. She found it hard enough to understand it herself let alone explain it to someone else. The only thing she could come up with was they were her parents, subconsciously she knew they would never hurt her.

"I was just so happy to see you both, and Dad, you were so upset, I didn't think. I guess having the comfort from you both is something that I need."

They sat in silence for a few moments, lost in their own thoughts.

Finally, Janet stood and asked, "Do you need anything from the shop?"

If Meredith was confused over the change of subject, she didn't show it. She shook her head and with a brief nod, her mum left. Meredith regarded her father who looked somewhat bewildered. She went and sat by him, their thighs touching, neither speaking for a few minutes.

"Honey, I am so sorry this is so hard on you. What can we do to make this better for you?"

"There's nothing you can do, Dad. I have a counsellor coming on Tuesday to see me and hopefully she will be able to help. Just you and Mum being here is enough. It's good to have mum's practical side here. I am concerned she might be burying her head in the sand and not dealing with all this, but I'm happy she's here helping." She reached out and took her father's hand, ignoring the surprise on his face when her fingers touched his. "You're my dad, you've always been there for me, guiding me, is my strength. I'm sorry this is hard for you, but I am going to be okay, I'll get through this."

"What does Kathleen say about all of this?"

"We haven't really spoken about it. She's picked up that I don't like to be touched and I think she's feeling a lot of rejection from me right now." Meredith drew in a breath. She ignored her father's grunt of derision. "I wouldn't necessarily say we're having problems, but we are definitely in different places right now. She's trying her best. I know this is difficult for her. I'm not sure how I would cope if my partner had been raped and tortured." Her father's hand tightened in her own. She didn't mean to say that last bit out loud and she could only imagine the images that flashed through his mind.

"I'm sorry, Dad."

"Don't you dare ever apologise for the crap that you've been through. That bastard hurt you through no fault of your own and I don't want to hear you ever say you're sorry for the things he did."

Her eyes teared, and they spilled down her cheeks. Gently, her father put his arms around her shoulders and hugged her close. Some of the tension and shame that were within her began to slip away. Finally, wrapped in the safety of her father's arms, she began to feel that maybe she could get over this, maybe she could heal.

†

Stephanie locked the door behind the last visitor, flipping the closed sign. She walked back over to where Joe sat behind the counter working on closing the till.

"Tell you what, Joe, it might have started out quiet this morning, but it soon picked up this afternoon."

"Yeah, if I haven't said it yet, I'll say it now, it's bloody good you came back when you did." Spring and summer were always their busiest times and they usually needed to work extra hours to cover the popularity of the gallery.

"Well, I'm glad I'm here to help you with your business. It's not like I've had a traumatic experience or anything."

Joe looked up from his accounting and caught the smirk on her face.

"You know, it's fine to joke about this and everything, but if you seriously need to talk, I'm here. And if you prefer something a bit more girly, I'm sure Fiona won't mind talking to you."

She looked away, thinking about his words. Ever since her accident as a child, things for her had never been normal. The brain injury had taken something away from her. She could understand people's emotions, could understand the way people felt, but she couldn't empathise with them. There was something missing within her, something she didn't know she needed. Like now, Joe obviously couldn't understand that she was fine. Yes, she did feel some anger that she was kidnapped, she didn't much like what happened, but she wasn't grieving, she wasn't upset. It was almost like the emotional switch within her brain had been switched off. The only time she could recall any sort of empathy or feeling was when West hurt Meredith. She didn't understand why that was, all she knew was Meredith had found a way inside her. Stephanie understood the concept of love, she thought she felt it for her mum, or at least should feel it for her mum, and she had strong feelings for Joe and Fiona, but the thing that was happening within her, her thoughts about Meredith, troubled her. She didn't care that she herself was brutalised, she only worried that Meredith had been.

She turned back to Joe, who was looking at her expectantly.

"I keep telling you this, Joe, I'm fine. You know it's not within me to have the sort of feelings you're expecting of me, they're just not there."

"It's okay, I just wanted to make the offer and it still stands."

She was about to reply when her mobile phone rang.

"Hello?"

"This is Detective Connor. I've been placed in charge of the Jameson West case. I wanted to make you aware of where things stand at present. He is still claiming his innocence, but we have officially charged him, he will be going to trial, and there is a good possibility you may need to give evidence."

"Sure, that's fine, let me know when you'll need me."

"Well, it may not be for a few months yet, but I shall keep you informed."

She hung up the phone and casually relayed what the officer had said to Joe. She shrugged at his questioning glance.

"The police have a lot of evidence against him, Joe. I can't see how he is claiming innocence, but I suppose he has to try."

She glanced at the clock hanging behind the counter and decided a few beers would be a good idea.

"Hey, do you fancy grabbing a few beers tonight?"

"I'd love to, but I need to get back and see Fi. We've hardly seen each other all week."

"Okay, cool. I'll see you later."

They said their goodbyes, and she went up to her apartment to get ready for a night out on her own. She might not have any real emotions going on inside her, but she still had thoughts, and those thoughts needed to be silenced.

†

Meredith hung up the phone and went back into the kitchen where Carrie stood at the sink washing dishes. She and Holly had come over as planned and Janet had cooked them the most delicious chilli Meredith had ever tasted. Holly was in the lounge with Meredith's parents discussing the advertising world they all worked in and Carrie and Meredith had offered to wash up. Meredith's phone had rung halfway through and she had gone to answer it.

"Who was that?" Carrie said, placing a saucepan onto the draining board.

"That was Detective Connor, he's the officer dealing with the kidnappings. Apparently, Jameson West is going to trial and I will have to give evidence."

Carrie stopped what she was doing. Wiping her hands on a tea towel, she turned to face her.

"That's insane! How the hell does he think he's going to get away with this?"

"The detective is confident that he won't and to be honest, I'm more concerned that I may have to leave the apartment."

"When do you start seeing the counsellor?"

"I have my first appointment on Tuesday." Meredith continued to dry the dishes and placed them in their respective cupboards. "I had a pretty bad anxiety attack this morning. Mum wanted to go to the shop and asked me to go with her and I froze. I was on the verge of passing out."

Carrie started towards her, her natural reaction to hug her, but Meredith turned away. She could see the hurt flash through Carrie's face, but she couldn't do anything about it, she was dismayed to feel the sting of tears on her cheeks.

"Oh, honey. Everything will be fine. No one can blame you for being apprehensive about people."

"But I know you're not going to hurt me, Carrie. Why can't everything just get back to normal?"

"You've only been home for a week. It's going to take time and we are all here to support you."

Stephanie's face came to Meredith's mind. She wondered who she had to support her. From what she could gather, she didn't have many people in her life.

They finished clearing up the kitchen and went back into the lounge where Harold was regaling Holly with tales of his early days at a car advertising firm. The evening continued pleasantly. Meredith looked between her parents and her friends, a warmth spreading through her body. It comforted her, and she knew she was safe.

Sometime later she was tucked up in bed, her laptop opened on her crossed legs. Her parents had retired to their room an hour earlier and Meredith had taken that time to relax in her own company. She had put it off for the last sixty minutes, but her curiosity finally got to her and she checked her email account. And there it was, an email from Stephanie.

Meredith, I'm pleased your parents arrived safely and you have their and Carrie's support. I find myself thinking of you quite often through the day and hoping that you are okay. I went back to work today as I couldn't stand being in the flat doing nothing. I've always been a doer. Joe still doesn't believe that I'm okay, but I was only gone a few weeks, you were there for months! I can see why this is hard for you, and I just wish there was something I could do to help you. I feel kind of useless. I'm going to have to end here as I've had quite a few beers and I'm afraid I may say something way too soppy and ridiculous. I hope everything goes okay with your counsellor and you find a way to deal with everything. Oh, and I also received a phone call from the police today. It looks like we'll be going to trial. I hope this news doesn't upset you too much.

Stephanie.

It was hard to decipher her words. She may have said she was okay with everything, but even with her medical history, she must be feeling something about what had happened. She may have only been there for a month, but that was a month of rape, torture, and starvation to name but a few. Meredith was with her during those long interminable hours, lying on that filthy mattress, talking about their lives. Stephanie might think she couldn't feel empathy, but Meredith knew she had shown it numerous times in that hellhole and in the emails she had sent. She knew there was a caring side to Stephanie and she wasn't going to let her hide from those feelings. She deserved to be looked after and cared for just as much as herself, and Meredith was going to see to that. Clearly, Joe cared about her, so she had at least one person in her corner. Now Stephanie had two.

Meredith closed her laptop without replying. She wanted time to think about what she was going to say and the right way to say it. She would sleep on it and, when she was refreshed in the morning, she would email her back.

Just as she closed her eyes it crossed her mind that she hadn't heard from Kathleen all day and hoped she had arrived in London safely. She grabbed her mobile phone on the bedside table, shot off a quick text saying that she missed her, and hoped she was safe. Only part of the text was true. She realised she hadn't missed her at all.

CHAPTER TEN

It was ten o'clock in the morning and Meredith sat at the kitchen table cogitating what to email Stephanie. Her parents had gone out for a few hours to do some shopping, and she was glad for the peace and quiet. She had enjoyed the evening with her friends and family, but she was exhausted. She was still underweight and fatigue set in easily. She was about to begin typing when she heard keys in the door and a few seconds later Kathleen came through. Her eyes darted about the room and then settled on Meredith. Meredith gasped at the sight before her. In all their time together, she didn't think she had ever seen Kathleen look so rough. Her hair was unkempt, and she had dark circles underneath her normally flawless eyes. Kathleen came fully into the kitchen but refused to meet her questioning gaze.

"Meredith, we need to talk."

"Come into the lounge and sit down. Can I get you a drink?"

"No, thank you, I'm fine."

Kathleen chose to sit in the armchair and Meredith wondered if this was an attempt to subconsciously distance herself. After she sat on the sofa Kathleen hesitantly looked at her.

"I'm not sure how to tell you this, but you need to know what I have done."

Meredith didn't say anything. She crossed one leg over the other and folded her hands in her lap, waiting for her to continue.

"I didn't go to London this weekend, I lied. I met a woman in a bar and we slept together last night."

"Oh." Meredith was unsure what to say. She knew they were having problems and that Kathleen was struggling with things, but she never thought in a million years Kathleen would cheat on her. "Tell me what's going on, Kath? I know you're struggling with everything that happened. Why didn't you talk to me?"

"You've been through absolute hell, and I felt like a coward for not being able to help you. Just the thought of the things he did to you drives me crazy. I'm not emotionally equipped to deal with this, Meredith, and we are not the same people any more. It's a callous thing to say, but you've changed, and I'm not the same person I was eight months ago either."

Meredith sat quietly, digesting all that Kathleen had said. She couldn't argue against the logic. They had changed, but Meredith had every right to change, she had been a victim of horrid abuse, and it wasn't something she was likely to get over any time soon.

"I know things have been a bit difficult for you, but it hasn't exactly been a picnic for me either. I'm sorry that I didn't come home and just magically fall back into the person I was. You have to understand the things I went through aren't something you just get over."

"Don't you think I know that? That's why I didn't say anything. I know you're facing a lot of demons and I knew my feelings didn't even compare to yours—"

"So, you thought you would just go fuck someone else?"

"It wasn't like that, Meredith. I met her earlier in the week and we got along well. It was nice to feel normal again, and not have to worry about kidnappers and rapists."

"Well, I'm glad you had a chance to escape for a while. I only wish I could afford myself the same luxury." Meredith rose from the sofa and headed toward the front door. "Get out. I can't believe after all of this time together you could do this."

Kathleen stood and met her at the threshold.

"I'm sorry. I didn't mean for this to happen. I do love you, but maybe it is best if we just had a break for a while."

"I'm not sure I can forgive you for this. I need some time. I need to deal with West first."

"I understand, but would it be okay if we kept in touch?"

"We'll see."

Meredith closed the door and went back to her laptop. Without thinking of what she was doing, she opened the email program and started to type.

Steph, I have been trying to find the right words to tell you how special you have become to me, but I truly have no idea where to start. I know you said you were doing okay, I really do hope that's true, but you need to know that I'm here if you ever want to talk.

I'm going to be a little bit selfish here and use you as a sounding board. Kathleen has just left after coming here to tell me that she slept with someone else last night. I could talk to Carrie about this, but I know what she would say, I don't think I could deal with her anger right now. And besides, it feels right talking to you, I feel close to you. Kathleen said she was finding it difficult to deal with her feelings about what had happened to me and she needed to escape for a while. We never particularly had a close relationship, but it has always been monogamous. I know I'm dealing with a lot of stuff right now, but she could have talked to me, we could have sorted this out. I can deal with the fact that she needed space, I would probably be the same, but to cheat on me? After the hell I've been through? It's just wrong. We're taking a break for a while, but I'm not sure if I will want her back or if she even wants to come back. She said the experience has changed me, I guess that's true. I'm still essentially the same person, my core values haven't changed, but I'm not as trusting or as open as I once was. I can't believe she just expected me to be normal after just two weeks of being home. I can't help the way I feel. We didn't ask for this, is it so hard for her just to try and give me time?

She sent the email and let out a breath. She didn't mean to get into everything about Kathleen, but she needed to talk to someone, to vent. She could have waited to speak to her parents, but being honest with herself, she wanted to speak to Stephanie.

She was about to close the lid when her computer dinged with an incoming email.

I can't believe she's done this to you! She's supposed to be your partner and support you through the good and the bad. I seriously want to come down there and shake her to make her realise what a callous thing she's done to you. I know you don't need my anger or my sympathies, but I am sending you a giant virtual hug. You are safe with me, Meredith, you can talk to me at any time. I'm going to give you my phone number which you can use whenever you like. If you are uncomfortable talking on the phone you can text me. I want you to feel you can get in contact with me at any time, and you can, Meredith, any time.

She didn't realise she was crying until a few drops of tears fell onto her keyboard. She wiped them away and sent a simple reply saying thank you. Her parents came through the door at that point and she scrubbed her hands over her face, gathering herself together. She hoped her parents didn't realise she'd been upset, she didn't want to deal with explaining Kathleen's betrayal just yet. She needed to figure these things out in her own mind first. And figure out the strange pull she felt toward Stephanie. She didn't understand it; however, she did know that she could feel the warmth of Stephanie's arms around her. It felt nice.

†

Sunday evening found Stephanie sitting at the bar of Hamilton's, a sports bar located around the corner from Joe's gallery, and it was their favourite place to unwind. The atmosphere was enjoyable, and even during football games, the crowd never got too rowdy. She sipped her beer, the cool liquid coating her dry throat. She was still reeling from Meredith's email that morning, and the revelation that

Kathleen had cheated on her. Stephanie's anger had always been the emotion she identified with most, and the fire in her belly now, and her trembling hands, paid testament to how furious she was.

"If Fiona went missing and what happened to me happened to her, what would you do?" she asked Joe. His face paled and she regretted the horrible images she had most likely put in his head. "Sorry, Joe. That was a stupid thing to say."

"No, it's okay. I just wasn't expecting it."

He took a gulp from his drink and she could see him giving serious thought to the question. He swivelled on his stool and faced her.

"I'm not sure how to answer that. I do know I would probably kill the bastard who took her. Aside from that, I don't know."

"I've been talking to Meredith, the woman who was in the room with me, and her partner cheated on her last night. She said she couldn't cope with the horrors Meredith had gone through."

"That sucks. I love Fiona and if she could never sleep with me again because of the shit that happened to her, I wouldn't care. She's my wife and there is more to a relationship than sex. I would like to think our relationship is built on more than just the physical."

Stephanie nodded. That was how she felt too. Surely the emotional connection was better than a sexual one. Not that she had any experience with long-term relationships, hell, she didn't even have any experience with a short-term one. She supposed she should be envious of people who had managed to find happiness with others, but as it was something she had never experienced for herself, she couldn't comment.

She was just about to reply to Joe when she caught sight of the television, mounted high above the bar on the back wall. The twenty-four-hour news channel was on and the scrolling reel along the bottom of the screen read: "Local man charged with nine counts of kidnap and four counts of murder." Stephanie gasped and nudged Joe on the shoulder.

"Jesus, Steph! You've made me spill my beer."

"It's him." She pointed to the picture that flashed on the screen behind the newsreader. He looked like any other normal-looking man. Close-cropped brown hair, brown eyes, five o'clock shadow. A birthmark, roughly the size of a strawberry, graced the man's neck and was the only distinguishable feature about him. "He looks so ordinary."

Joe placed his hand on her forearm and squeezed gently. "Are you okay?"

She noted the concern in his eyes and felt blessed she had him in her life.

"I'm fine, Joe. It's good to finally put a face to the monster that hurt Meredith and all those women."

"He hurt you too, Steph," Joe said carefully.

"I know that! I just meant..." She shook her head, not sure why she couldn't relate her own experience with Jameson West to that of the others.

"I need to make a call."

She left the pub through the back door and took huge gulps of the evening air. The smell of the day's rubbish filled her nostrils as she leaned up against the wall. She opened her contact list on her phone, glad she had all her numbers backed up to the Cloud and scrolled down until she found the number she was looking for. A husky voice answered.

"Hey, Claire, it's Steph,"

"I wondered when you were going to call. It's been a while."

She thought back to the last time she had seen Claire. It was over eight months ago when they had hooked up in the back room of a club. She had been aroused at the sight of Claire's lithe body, swaying on the dance floor to the pulsing beat, wearing a skimpy little red dress. They had known each other for three years now and Claire took great delight in teasing her every time they met up for drinks. They were friends with benefits, but most of the time, Stephanie didn't much enjoy the benefits. Tonight, though, she needed a distraction from the thoughts that plagued her of how inadequate and abnormal she felt in her own life.

"Sorry, Claire, but I've been crazy busy." She supposed she should tell her about the kidnapping, but honestly, it was the last thing she wanted to talk about. "I was hoping we could meet up, if you're up for it."

Claire chuckled down the line, her laugh deep and gravelly.

"Sure, babe. You know where I am."

Stephanie hung up and headed back into the bar. She said her goodbyes to Joe, feigning a headache, and was out the door. The guilt of lying to Joe tugged at her, but sometimes, escaping was the only way she could deal with her lack of coping skills.

CHAPTER ELEVEN

Stephanie was upstairs in her flat getting ready for bed. It was Thursday night and she and Joe had gone through a long, hard day at work. It had been unusually busy, but Joe welcomed the business. She grabbed a towel on her way out of her minuscule bathroom and vigorously rubbed it over her hair as she walked into her bedroom. She threw the towel on the floor, and as she began to step into her sleep shorts, her mobile phone rang. She didn't recognise the number but considering it was nearly ten o'clock at night, she thought it might be something important.

"Hello?" There was silence on the other end for a few moments and her heart rate kicked up a beat, thinking that somehow Jameson West had gotten her number. Her relief was palpable when Meredith's voice came down the line.

"Hi, Stephanie. It's me, Meredith."

She sat on her bed, bewildered. She hadn't thought Meredith would use her phone number, preferring to email back and forth, but Stephanie was glad she had.

"Hi, Mare. Is everything okay? Not that I mind you calling me, it's just it's late and you haven't phoned before." Stephanie could hear Meredith's ragged breathing coming down the line, something was wrong.

"I'm sorry, it's late, I should let you sleep."

Stephanie rushed in to stop Meredith from disconnecting. "It's fine. Talk to me."

"I guess I'm just feeling a little out of sorts tonight. The counsellor gave me some good exercises to do, to help with my anxiety and things, but I don't know, I guess I'm just afraid."

"Are your parents still there?"

"Yes. They've turned in for the night, but it's not them I wanted to speak to. It's hard for me to tell them how I'm feeling. I know they would understand and sympathise and help me, but it's not the same. They weren't there. I don't want to have to explain everything in detail to make them understand."

Stephanie could sense her panic. It tore her up to know that Meredith was struggling so much.

"I know this is difficult for you, but don't forget you've only had one session with your counsellor, it'll just take time. I do know how you feel, Meredith. I feel the same way with Joe, except he is expecting me to break down at any minute and turn into a blubbering mess. He knows how I am, and it's just not going to happen." She shifted up the bed and rested her back on the headboard. "I saw Jameson West's face on the news the other day and I felt nothing for myself.

Joe was shocked that I was so angry over what he had done to you and the others but had no concern for myself. I guess he thinks that I'm suppressing it, perhaps he's right."

"Stephanie, I don't think there is anything wrong with you. Maybe that doctor was right, and on some level, you close yourself off to feeling anything that can hurt you. That's something only you can answer, and if it's something you want to explore, I'll help if I can."

"After I saw him on the news, I phoned an old friend. We had sex." She waited for Meredith's reply, but all she heard was silence on the other end. "See, that's weird, right? I just spent five weeks being abused and tortured and I have absolutely no problem with going out and having sex with a woman just for the fun of it. Except it wasn't fun, I just felt empty, just as empty as I did with West."

"Perhaps that proves my point. Look, we all deal with grief in different ways. I think losing your mother affected you more than you think. I hate to see you going through all this and I'm concerned that one of these days you'll have a breakdown and it will all come out at once."

Stephanie listened to Meredith's words, thinking perhaps she might be right, and maybe she should see her own therapist. She also noticed Meredith hadn't commented that Stephanie had chosen to have sex with a woman. It wasn't the first time Stephanie had been with Claire, and she had told Meredith before that she slept with men and women. The confession obviously didn't faze her. She idly wondered if she had chosen a woman because of West.

"I don't know, Mare. Anyway, don't worry, it's something I will have to figure out. You didn't call me to talk about me so let's get back to you."

"Actually, you've helped me take my mind off things for a while. It's nice to hear your voice again, I just wish we hadn't met under such awful circumstances. I think we could have been great friends."

"That can still happen. Just because we met in a horrific way doesn't mean we can't still be friends." Stephanie was sure what she was about to propose was going to sound weird, but she didn't care, she needed this to happen. "It's my birthday in a few weeks, I'm going to be turning thirty. Apart from having drinks with Joe, I'm completely free. How about if I came down and visited you?"

"Do you think that's a little strange?"

"No, I don't. I'm not sure about you, but something happened to me in that room, and I feel connected to you. I know it was probably the stress of being there, but I can't help but want to get to know you better. I find myself worrying about you and wanting to know if you're okay. I know this is probably a bad idea, and seeing me might bring back flashbacks or whatever, but I need to see you, Meredith."

She was greeted by silence again. She feared she had gone too far, said too much, but she couldn't make herself take back the words. She did need to see Meredith. Stephanie had always been content with her life, and her lack of emotions never really bothered her before. Since meeting Meredith, and going through what they had together, she now found her lack of feelings troubling. Only when she thought of Meredith did she feel anything other than empty. Meredith somehow had opened something in her and she needed to find out what that was and why it was Meredith who had done this. She also needed to make sure Meredith was okay. She obviously wasn't coping with everything very well, and Stephanie hoped she could somehow help her.

"I'm not sure that's an entirely good idea," Meredith finally said, "but I find myself wanting to see you, too. If you're sure, I would be happy to celebrate your birthday with you."

Relief spread through Stephanie's body and she sank back into her bed, relaxing her muscles. She didn't realise how tense she had been waiting for her answer.

"I'm sure. Thanks, Mare."

"No, thank you. I'm glad I called. I'll leave you to the rest of your evening. I'll speak to you soon."

They said their goodnights and Stephanie finished drying her hair, thinking about the prospect of seeing Meredith again.

†

It had been just over a week since Meredith had spoken to Stephanie on the phone. They had emailed a few times since then, mainly checking in with each other, making sure they were okay. She continued to see a counsellor every few days, and she found it was helping her to cope with everything. Kathleen had texted her a couple of times, asking if she was okay, and each time Meredith replied with a simple, "Yes, I'm okay." She still hadn't examined her feelings for Kathleen, not properly anyway. She could admit she still loved her, but she knew she was not in love with her. At some point they would have to sit down together and have a proper talk about it all, but for now, Meredith wanted to concentrate on getting back to normal.

Larry had been by to see her at the beginning of the week to discuss some business matters, and Meredith found herself wanting to go back to work. She knew she wouldn't cope doing her usual sixty-hour week, but she hoped to at least go in on a part-time basis. With her counsellor's help, and her parents,' she had managed to leave her apartment on a few occasions. She didn't go anywhere major, just to the local shop and to her counsellor's office. It was baby steps, but she was proud that she was improving.

She looked up from the local newspaper she was reading as her dad came into the lounge.

"Hey, Dad. Is Mum not back from the shops yet?"

"Not yet, honey. You know what she's like when she's let loose, always distracted by the shiny things."

Meredith laughed at her dad's characterisation of her mother. It was true that her mum liked to shop. She could be gone for hours looking at nothing in particular. It drove them both mad when they went with her. Meredith could understand why her dad never went often.

"I've just had a call from one of my managers in New York," he continued. "He said there are a few problems back there that need to be sorted out and wants to know when I'll be coming back."

She could see the indecision in her father's eyes. There was no way he would leave her if he felt she still needed him. If she asked, her parents would probably stay here indefinitely, but she knew that wasn't fair to them. They had a business to run, and even though they were in their early sixties there was no danger of them slowing down anytime soon.

She took her father's hand and gently ran her fingers over the faint blue lines of his veins running through his tanned skin.

"Dad, the last three weeks of you being here have been amazing. You know I miss you and mum every day and I wish you lived closer. But I understand you have a business to run and I wouldn't want to keep you from that. I'm doing a lot better now, the counselling is helping, and Carrie and Holly have been wonderful. There's nothing more you can do for me here that you can't do from over there. We can Skype and email and obviously we have the phone. I'll be fine. I don't want your business collapsing just because I'm clingy and emotionally unstable. You should go."

"Meredith, there is no way we can leave you just yet. You're not well enough."

"Dad, there's nothing physically wrong with me anymore. Yes, I have some scars on the outside and I'm still underweight, but my issues are on the inside, and as much as you would like to, you can't help me with that. Only I can sort that out, and I am."

Her dad didn't speak, he just looked at her the way he always did, eyes full of warmth and love. He moved closer on the couch and opened his arms and she didn't hesitate to move into them. He held her tight and she inhaled the smell of his cologne, committing it to memory. She felt his tears on her neck and she couldn't help but shed a few of her own.

"It's okay, Dad. I love you. Thank you for being here."

They sat together for a long while, neither one speaking, just enjoying being together after all the hardships that had befallen Meredith recently.

She turned to her dad and asked, "When do you leave?"

"I can probably get us on a flight tomorrow."

Meredith nodded.

"You make sure you call us at any time if you need anything. Your mother won't leave unless she knows she can trust you to keep in touch. We don't want you to be in pain anymore and if you're going to sit here on your own without speaking to anybody, she won't go."

"I promise, Dad. Please don't worry, I'll be fine."

"Don't be silly, of course we worry. And what's with Kathleen not being here?"

"Please, Dad, I don't want to talk about Kathleen."

He looked away and gave a firm nod. He seemed to understand there were some things Meredith would never talk to him about, and her relationship with Kathleen was one of them.

The key turning in the lock made them both turn toward the door as her mother walked in carrying nothing except her handbag.

"Mum, you've been gone three hours and you haven't bought anything?" Meredith chuckled.

"There was nothing that I fancied, dear. And besides, I enjoy looking."

Meredith looked back to her dad and they both shared a conspiratorial smile.

CHAPTER TWELVE

"So, how does it feel to be thirty?" Fiona asked.

"About the same as twenty-nine did." Stephanie looked across the small oak dining table at her friend and smiled.

They were sitting in Joe and Fiona's dining room having just finished eating a lovely roast cooked by Fiona. She was an excellent cook, and any opportunity Stephanie had to sample her food, she took it.

Fiona and Joe had been married for twelve years and were high school sweethearts. Stephanie had only ever known them together and they always seemed so in love and so happy. She could not remember a time when Joe had ever said anything bad about Fiona or mentioned that they had argued. They were the perfect couple.

Joe entered the room, having just taken the plates to the kitchen. He sat down and topped off their glasses with the deep-plum Rioja Stephanie had brought with her. She could still smell the roast lamb in the air, and coupled with the wine, the odours sent Stephanie's senses into overdrive. The tastes and aromas were a very pleasing combination.

"You sure you wouldn't prefer to go out?" Joe asked her.

"Nah, I told you, this is exactly what I want. We're always in the pub. It's nice to have a civilised meal, with beautiful company." She smiled at Fiona and winked.

"Stop hitting on my wife."

Fiona was a beautiful woman; her honey golden hair was braided into a French twist. Her blue eyes were always warm and caring, and she had the sweetest smile. Joe was a very lucky man.

"I wouldn't stand a chance, Joe, not with you around."

A stab of loneliness hit her square in the chest as she witnessed the look of admiration Joe directed at Fiona, and Fiona's answering blush. Ever since speaking with Meredith on the phone the other week, Stephanie found herself more aware of her emotions. She didn't like it. Never had she had to put up with feelings like jealousy, loneliness, and wistfulness. On more than one occasion she would be busy at work and suddenly, these random feelings would hit her. Usually they were accompanied by a picture of Meredith in her mind. She found she was looking forward to seeing her again, she couldn't wait. A small grin crossed her face when she realised she would be seeing her in less than thirty-six hours.

"What's that look for?" Joe asked.

"Sorry, just thinking."

She debated whether to tell Joe and Fiona about her plans for the coming weekend. She'd already asked Joe for some time off and she had sidestepped his question about why she needed it, saying it was for personal reasons. He hadn't questioned her further and she assumed he probably thought it was due to the kidnapping. She glanced at them, back and forth, and decided to tell them the truth. They were her friends, the only ones she had, and they would be supportive of her, she knew it.

"Actually, there is something you might want to know. Friday afternoon I will be catching the train down to Bristol." At their raised eyebrows she continued. "I'm going down there for a few days to spend some time with Meredith."

Joe frowned at her and she could see him trying to decipher who Meredith was. She knew the exact time he realised it, his eyes went wide, his mouth forming the shape of an O.

"Who is Meredith?" Fiona asked.

Joe found his voice and said, "Meredith is the woman who was locked up with Stephanie."

Fiona's gaze darted from her husband and back to her. She knew she looked guilty. She didn't know why, she wasn't doing anything wrong, but for some reason she couldn't bring herself to look her friends in the eye.

"I know it probably seems weird to you, but she's having a hard time, and we kind of miss each other."

"Stephanie," Fiona said, "it's not that it's weird, it's just, how can I put it? I guess really the question is why?"

Stephanie considered her understanding blue eyes. Fiona placed a hand on top of hers, giving it a slight squeeze, silently asking her to continue. She shrugged and shook her head slightly.

"I can't really speak for Meredith, but for me, something happened inside that room." She glared at Joe when he snorted. "Obviously I'm not referring to the bad stuff that happened." She looked back to Fiona. "We were together for five weeks, and in that time, we talked. A lot. I liked her and she was the first person I can recall who has gotten past my defences. You and Joe are my family, and of course I love you both, but somehow, she's managed to bring out feelings in me I never thought capable of feeling. I don't know if that's because of what happened to me when we were there, or because of who she is, but this is something I need to figure out. I can't stop thinking about her and wondering if she's okay. I'm a little adrift here. I've never had so many thoughts and feelings happen to me before."

"Do you think this is an attachment to her because of what happened?" Fiona asked.

"I don't know, you could be right. The only thing I know for sure is that I need to see her. She wants to see me too."

She could feel Joe's eyes boring into her. He clearly couldn't hold his silence any more.

"What?"

He shook his head and folded his arms across his chest. "I'm sorry, Steph, but I don't think seeing her is the best thing for you, or her. You went through some terrible things together and maybe seeing each other isn't the wisest thing to do. If she's having as hard a time as you say, do you really think seeing you would be good for her? It could cause all kinds of flashbacks and panic attacks."

He was right, this was a bad idea, but she had no choice, she needed to see her.

"I understand what you're saying, Joe, but this is something I need to do. Moreover, I want to do this."

Fiona stood and came around to her side of the table. She took her hands and tugged, pulling her up.

She hugged Stephanie close. "Do what you need to do, we are here if you need us."

Stephanie sighed, relieved that she had at least Fiona's support. She broke the embrace and looked at Joe, who was still sitting at the table, arms folded with a scowl on his face.

"I don't agree with this, Steph, but Fiona is right. You are my best friend and when this all goes wrong, and it will go wrong, we'll be here."

Stephanie nodded, understanding Joe's reservations, but immensely pleased he still supported her. She sat back down and took a large gulp from her glass. Friday evening couldn't come soon enough.

†

Meredith pushed the shopping trolley down the vegetable aisle of the local supermarket. It was early Friday afternoon and Stephanie would be arriving later that night. She wasn't sure what Stephanie had in mind for her visit, but Meredith wanted to at least cook her a birthday meal. The only problem was she had no idea what kind of foods Stephanie liked. She had been wandering around for the best part of an hour now, and so far, all she had in her trolley was a dozen eggs, a tin of peaches, and some fresh basil. What she thought she was going to cook with those ingredients, she had no idea.

She put down the fresh cauliflower she held in her hand and took her phone out of her pocket. She should call Stephanie and ask what she liked, but she wanted it to be a surprise. So instead she dialled Carrie's number. Her friend answered on the third ring.

"Hey, Mare, how are things?"

"Everything is going well. It's been nice having the house to myself since my parents left. Obviously, I miss them, but it's been good to get back to a quasi-routine."

Meredith had filled her days with seeing her counsellor and working on some projects for work. Getting back into a routine had helped with her anxiety and she felt better within herself.

"I do need your help with something though." She had not yet told Carrie of Stephanie's impending visit. She idly wondered if doing it now, in the middle of the supermarket, would be a wise thing to do. "Stephanie is coming down from York tonight and it's her birthday. I want to cook her a surprise meal but have no idea what she likes."

Carrie cleared her throat and Meredith's heart rate sped up. If she wasn't careful, she would be having a panic attack in the middle of the vegetables.

"I think there are some things you have neglected to tell me, Meredith, in the last few times we've spoken. As soon as she leaves, whenever that is, you need to call me and I will come around to see you. We need to have a talk."

Meredith sighed, realising she had made a mistake. Carrie was her friend and she should have confided in her. She was about to apologise when Carrie continued.

"Don't sweat it for now, but we will need to talk about this. As for what to cook? I assume as it's a surprise you don't want to ask her what it is that she likes, I would just suggest buying a takeaway. You could still do whatever it is you plan to do with table settings and such, and then just have her pick what takes her fancy."

"Yes, I think you're right." She walked over to the wine aisle and began perusing the Chiantis and Pinot Noirs. "I'm sorry I haven't mentioned her visit to you, but I didn't know how to bring it up. We have been emailing back and forth and talking over the last few weeks. We find we have some things in common. I think we both want to check on each other, make sure we're okay." She put two bottles of red in her trolley and took out the few items she had selected for the meal, plonking them on a nearby shelf.

"It's fine, I promise. But we do need to have a talk when I see you next."

"Thank you, Carrie. I'm not sure how to explain this, but I'm looking forward to seeing her."

"What time is she arriving? And how does Kathleen feel about this?"

Meredith bit her lip, wincing when she realised she hadn't told Carrie about her separation from Kathleen or about Kathleen's cheating. This was another berating she would likely receive from Carrie.

"Kathleen doesn't know she's coming. In fact, I haven't spoken with Kathleen for a couple of weeks. We've sort of gone on a break."

"What?"

Meredith could hear the hurt and confusion in Carrie's voice, and she felt like the worst friend ever.

"What is going on with you, Meredith? I know you have gone through a lot of stuff recently, but surely you could have spoken to me about this. I could have helped you."

"I'm sorry. You're right, and I promise I will make it up to you. A lot is going on and I just didn't want to deal with it."

"I need to go, I have a call waiting. Call me when she leaves."

Carrie disconnected without saying goodbye, and Meredith was disgusted with herself for hurting her best friend. She stood in line at the checkout and a burly man joined the queue behind her. He stood a little too close for her liking and she felt her palms start to sweat. She could feel her adrenaline pumping through her veins and wished the checkout operator would hurry up. She glanced over her shoulder and, for just a second, she thought she recognised the eyes of Jameson West.

She quickly paid for her purchases and rushed for the exit.

She got inside the car she had newly leased, slammed and locked the door, and gripped the steering wheel tightly. Her breathing was coming in short gasps and she couldn't settle her heart rate. Clearly, she wasn't as adjusted to being outside as she thought. She started to count out loud, trying to control her breaths, and concentrated on the exercises her counsellor had given her. She needed to get this under control. She would not have a panic attack in the middle of the car park.

CHAPTER THIRTEEN

Stephanie stood outside the nondescript door of Meredith's top floor apartment. It was eight-thirty at night and she had spent the last few hours on the train and in a taxi to get here. She was tired but excited to be seeing Meredith again. She took a deep breath and knocked on the door. A few moments later, Meredith stood in front of her, smiling widely, making the skin around her eyes crinkle. Stephanie was mesmerised. Meredith wore loose linen trousers and a pale green tank top, which complemented the red curls brushing her shoulders. She had put on weight in the weeks since Stephanie had seen her, and her skin had lost the deathly pallor she had in the hospital. She looked vibrant and healthy.

"Hi," Meredith said.

"Hi."

They stood looking at each other and Stephanie didn't know how to proceed. Meredith saved her wondering as she opened the door wider and pulled her into a hug. Stephanie's arms came around the smaller woman and she inhaled the sweet citrus aroma of her hair.

"It is so good to see you," Stephanie whispered.

Meredith stood back from her, and after grasping her hand, pulled her into her home. She took in all the details on her way through, impressed by Meredith's choice of decor. It had the feeling of comfort and cosiness but was big enough in size to not feel crowded. Meredith kept pulling her along until she stopped in a mid-sized room which was decorated in a similar fashion to the rest of the apartment, complete with double bed, small wardrobe, and dresser.

Meredith turned to regard her, and Stephanie lost herself in the magnetic blue eyes. She didn't know what was happening, she didn't recognize the tightening of her stomach or why she felt hotter than normal, nor the unfathomable reason why her palms were sweating. Stephanie was captivated by her beauty and she thanked God that Meredith had made it out safely.

"I know we didn't discuss where you would be staying," Meredith said, "but I just assumed you would stay here."

She motioned around the room and Stephanie could not help but smile at Meredith's apparent nervousness. She could see a faint tremble in her body and the blush that highlighted her cheeks.

"This is fine, thank you." She took the rucksack off her back and placed it at the foot of the bed. She stretched her back muscles and was dismayed when she felt a yawn happening. She blushed. "Sorry, it's been a long journey."

"That's okay." Meredith grabbed her hand again leading her back into the lounge. "Please, take a seat."

Stephanie did as asked watching as Meredith went over to the fireplace. There was a small package sitting on top wrapped in pink paper. Meredith picked it up and brought it back to where she sat. She held out the gift.

"Happy birthday!"

Stephanie took the package, her eyes wide. She never expected to receive anything. Her birthday was three days ago, and she had just assumed Meredith would have no reason to buy her a gift.

"You didn't need to do this." Seeing Meredith's smile fade and the excitement in her eyes dim, she added, "but thank you. This is very thoughtful of you."

Meredith sat down next to her.

"It's not much, just a little something."

Stephanie began to unwrap the gift and noticed Meredith fidgeting in her seat, her nerves now palpable. She placed a hand on her thigh and was pleased when she stilled. She was stunned when she unwrapped the gift. Lying on a small velvet pillow was a black thong necklace with a compass charm attached to it. She ran her finger over the design and looked up at Meredith.

"So, you don't get lost and can always find your way." The words were whispered and filled with sincerity.

Stephanie had never received anything as thoughtful and special as this was. Her eyes filled with tears, and after rubbing them away, she said, "Thank you." She moved in to hug her.

Meredith came toward her, and as Stephanie leaned in to kiss her cheek, Meredith moved her head in the same direction, and she inadvertently kissed Stephanie on the lips.

Her eyes went wide at the feel of Meredith's lips against her own. She sprang back into the sofa. She sat there blinking rapidly, stunned at the adrenaline that was running through her body.

Meredith recovered first and stood. She ran a hand through her hair and went into the kitchen. A few moments later she came back through to the lounge holding a bottle of wine in one hand, two glasses in the other, and what looked like way too many restaurant menus held against her side with her elbow.

"I was going to cook you something to celebrate you turning thirty, but I realised I had no idea what it is you like to eat."

Stephanie was glad the confusing moment was swept away. It was likely that Meredith didn't feel anything from that split-second of contact, but for Stephanie, her whole world had just been blown apart. She had never felt anything like the connection she had felt from Meredith's lips on her own.

Meredith settled the glasses and the wine on the coffee table in front of them and handed her the stack of menus.

"I thought maybe we could just order something and that way you will not have to be subjected to my awful cooking. We can sit and catch up while waiting for the food to arrive." She handed her a glass of wine. "You do like wine, don't you?"

"Yes, thank you."

"Of course, if you are too tired, we can always call it a night and catch up tomorrow."

"No, I'm fine. It's still early and I'm starving."

To be totally honest with herself, she could have done with a nap when she had arrived, but her adrenaline was still coursing through her veins. She didn't think she would be able to sleep for hours yet, and a few glasses of wine were exactly what was needed to clear her head.

†

So far, the evening had been a pleasant one, and Meredith found Stephanie to be an engaging company. They had just finished clearing up the remnants of their Indian curry and were sitting together on the sofa finishing off the second bottle of wine Meredith had purchased earlier that day. She enjoyed the light buzz that was running through her body from the alcohol. She had been nervous about Stephanie's visit all day, but sitting here now, talking about her work, she felt relaxed. In the back of her mind, she could not help but think of the moment earlier when Stephanie had opened her birthday present. She had wanted to buy her a gift but was not sure what would be appropriate for someone who was only just becoming your friend.

She had seen the necklace a few days earlier as she passed by the jewellery shop near her office. The compass caught her eye instantly. She deviated from her journey home and pushing her anxiety away at entering an unfamiliar property, she went into the shop and asked to see the necklace. It was beautiful. She knew it was the perfect gift. Stephanie had expressed to her before that she felt lost in her own life, with no direction as to where she was headed, floundering in her emotions, and Meredith hoped this small gesture would bring her at least a modicum of comfort.

She also remembered the brush of Stephanie's lips against her own. It had been by accident that Meredith had turned toward her. When their lips met, she felt sucker punched. Never in all her time with Kathleen had she felt the instant rush of arousal the tiny kiss from Stephanie brought her. She was shocked her body even knew how to respond to physical intimacy, or even that arousal could be something in her future. She could hardly tolerate Kathleen touching her and even hugs from her parents still felt uncomfortable. She didn't want to examine why Stephanie had the power to breach her insecurities and scale her walls.

She shook her head when she realized Stephanie had asked her a question that she missed completely. Her cheeks grew hot and she felt the blush work its way up her skin.

"Sorry, what?"

"I said, how is everything going with your counsellor?"

"She has been wonderful and helped me a lot. I find I can keep control of my panic attacks by using the exercises she has given me. I am getting better at going outside, and hopefully tomorrow I can show you a little bit of where I live."

"That would be great."

They grew silent, each seemingly lost in her own thoughts. Stephanie turned her head to the side, studying her face. Meredith felt her blush returning.

"What is it?" she asked softly.

"Nothing. Just admiring how well you have healed physically. You look really good, Meredith."

Meredith briefly closed her eyes, letting Stephanie's deep voice coat her insides. She studied Stephanie's face, which was inches from her own. She gently traced her finger over the scar on her forehead, remembering the first day they had met in that room, the blood that had coated her face, and Stephanie's confusion over what was happening and where she was. Meredith was momentarily lost back in that

102

moment. She shook her head, clearing the images from her mind. She traced the scar again and allowed her hand to rest against Stephanie's cheek. The scar was not as angry-looking as the last time she had seen it in the hospital. It had faded to a pink line, but it did nothing to detract from her handsomeness. Her green eyes shone with the effects of the wine and she looked truly relaxed.

Meredith felt her pulse quicken.

"You're not doing too badly yourself," she heard herself say.

Her hand continued its journey down Stephanie's neck and stopped on the compass that she now wore. Stephanie's hand came up and held Meredith's own against her throat, trapping the compass underneath it.

"Thank you, Meredith. It seems stupid to say, but I am glad you were there with me. I'm not sure how I would have made it through without you. And how you made it for months, I will never know."

Stephanie's hand was warm against her own and Meredith marvelled at the heartbeat she could feel pulsing underneath her fingertips, so full of life. She didn't know what was happening, but she felt the tug of connection. She couldn't explain it and she felt no need to examine the feelings that were running rampant through her body. She just enjoyed the moment, her time with Stephanie was the most relaxing and nerve-wracking she could recall spending with anyone before. She did not want the night to end, and that thought alone was reason enough to go to bed now.

Instead she said, "You have no idea how happy I am we got out of there alive. I can't believe we have to go to court and face that asshole, and I hope he doesn't get away with what he did to us."

103

"He won't, I promise."

She closed her eyes, praying Stephanie was right. There was no way she would cope if he got away with his crimes. It was all good and well, moving on with your life when you knew your tormenter was locked up, it was quite another to have them walking around, living life free, looking for other victims, thinking he was invincible.

Meredith shivered at the thought.

"You okay?" Stephanie asked, moving her hand to Meredith's and entwining their fingers.

"Yes. Just thinking about West."

"Don't," Stephanie said as she held her hand tighter. "Please do not give that bastard another thought until we have to. The court case will come soon enough."

Meredith could see the anguish on Stephanie's face and hated herself for putting the anger in her at the mention of his name. She shifted closer, and without giving it a thought, she rested her head on her shoulder, comforted when Stephanie's arm came around her and pulled her closer. It felt good to be this close to her again as if her world righted itself just being in her arms.

"Let's not talk about him," she said. "This weekend is about celebrating your birthday and getting to know each other."

Stephanie didn't answer, she just hugged her tighter.

†

Stephanie wasn't sure what had awakened her. She pressed the illumination button on her watch and saw it had just gone two o'clock in the morning. She rolled over onto her back, her eyes adjusting to the darkness of the room. She strained her ears, listening to the unfamiliar sounds of the house settling. A blood-curdling scream boomed through the walls, and Stephanie threw off her duvet, sprang from the bed, and rushed out the bedroom door. The scream came again, and without giving it a thought, she barged into Meredith's bedroom.

Meredith was on her back thrashing around, gripped in an apparent nightmare. Her duvet was on the floor and her pillows were strewn about. Stephanie came closer and called her name, trying to wake her. Stephanie's blood pumped hard through her veins, her panic rising. God only knew the horror Meredith was reliving.

She needed to get her out of there.

She sat on the bed, mindful of Meredith's swinging arms, and said her name again. She still didn't wake. Stephanie didn't want to hold Meredith down for fear she might think there was an intruder in the apartment or make the nightmare worse.

She glanced around the room and saw a half-full glass of water on the bedside table. Feeling guilty of what she was about to do, she picked it up and tipped it over Meredith's face, the effect was instant.

Meredith woke with a start, she sat bolt upright, her frightened gaze frantically searching around the room. They finally settled on Stephanie, who sat next to her.

"Stephanie?" Her voice was ragged as she struggled to catch her breath.

"It's okay, you were having a nightmare." Stephanie held one of her hands and gently rubbed her back, trying to calm her.

After a few minutes, Meredith's breathing returned to normal and she scrubbed a hand over her face.

"Jesus, I haven't had a dream that bad in weeks."

Stephanie could see the tremors still running through Meredith's body and she feared it may have been her own arrival today, and the talk they had about West earlier, that had brought on the nightmare.

"I think maybe Joe was right. He said that if we saw each other again we could possibly trigger flashbacks." She shook her head, angry with herself for causing Meredith's fear. "I am so sorry. I was so selfish coming here without thinking what this could do to you psychologically." A small tear escaped her eye and she felt Meredith shift on the bed. Her cool fingers wiped away a tear as she settled her hand on Stephanie's cheek.

"Oh, honey. This was not you. I have been having nightmares on and off since I have been home. You being here didn't cause this. And I wanted you here just as much as you wanted to be here. Please don't blame yourself."

Stephanie appreciated the words, but she still felt responsible. Deciding there was nothing she could do about any of this now, she stood from the bed and folded her arms across her chest.

"You might want to get changed. I could only wake you by throwing water on you."

Meredith looked down at herself as if only now realising she was wet. Stephanie's eyes followed her movements and in the dim light she could see the protrusions of Meredith's nipples pushing against the fabric of the pale-yellow tank top she wore. As she glanced back up into Meredith's face, she was dismayed to see Meredith staring at her intently. And now she really hated herself. Not only had she caused Meredith to have a horrible nightmare, but she was also now leering at her and had been caught in the process.

"Sorry. I'll just leave you to change." She left as quickly as her feet, and shame could carry her.

She flopped face first onto her own bed and groaned into the pillow. She was in danger of alienating Meredith, the one person she felt a strong connection with, aside from Joe, and the only person to bring out any kind of feelings in her. The last thing Meredith needed right now was Stephanie acting like a horny teenager around her. She couldn't help herself, though. Meredith was a beautiful woman, and for the first time in her life, Stephanie was attracted to someone physically and emotionally. She had always thought she was faulty. She could appreciate a good-looking guy or a pretty woman, but she never felt any stirrings of arousal. She'd slept with people plenty of times, but usually when drunk or purely just for the release of the energy which built up within her over time. She never felt any attachment to the people she had sex with and she was okay with that. She just assumed her lack of feelings toward people meant she would never feel the intensely deep passion other people felt. But being with Meredith was changing all that. They had grown close whilst trapped in that room, and with every email sent between them Stephanie became more connected to her.

She needed to talk to Fiona. She couldn't deal with this on her own and no way in hell was she going to mention her growing feelings to Meredith. It was likely this was all due to the trauma they had experienced together. She needed to get her raging emotions back under control. Just because Meredith was the one to bring these feelings to the surface didn't mean she was the one they should be directed toward.

With a plan settled in her mind, she decided to go back to sleep. She was about to settle under her duvet when there was a quiet knock on her door. She went to the door and opened it.

"Hi," Meredith said, shyly looking at the floor.

"Hi."

Meredith had changed into a dry tank top and shorts and Stephanie could not help but notice the dark circles that ringed her eyes, even in the wan light.

"This is going to sound really weird, but I couldn't fall back to sleep. I was kind of hoping I could stay with you."

Meredith's nervousness was not hard to miss, Stephanie thought the blush tingeing her cheeks was endearing. She shook her head at her thoughts, stepped back from the door, and motioned her inside with a tilt of her head. This was a bad idea, but she couldn't turn her away.

"Of course, that's fine."

Meredith brushed passed her and went around to the other side of the bed. Without looking at Stephanie she climbed in and settled on her left side, facing the wall. Stephanie shut the door and joined her on the mattress. Being this close to Meredith was nothing new. They had spent a lot of time sharing the same space, but in filthier conditions. Sleeping next to Meredith should be easy.

It was not.

She could feel the heat of Meredith's skin radiating between the few inches of space that separated them, and her sweet scent tickled Stephanie's nostrils. This was a different kind of torture, being here like this, but one she found she didn't mind.

"Thanks for this, Steph," Meredith whispered as she turned over and faced her.

Stephanie's pulse quickened when she felt Meredith rest her head on her shoulder and laid her arm across her waist.

Involuntarily, her own hand settled on her arm, holding her in place. She could feel Meredith's breath flutter against her neck, becoming deeper as she relaxed into sleep. She hoped she herself would fall asleep just as quickly; however, lying here holding Meredith in her arms, Stephanie doubted that would happen.

CHAPTER FOURTEEN

Meredith placed a cup of coffee in front of Stephanie where she sat at the dining table. She grabbed a plate of toast and butter from the worktop and settled down next to her. They had been awake for an hour now, but neither one had mentioned the nightmare from last night or waking up this morning tangled in each other. She hated to think what Stephanie thought of her for suggesting they sleep together, but she didn't care if she looked needy or clingy. Her nightmare had shaken her and only the closeness of Stephanie was going to put her at ease.

"I'm sorry if I made you uncomfortable last night," she said tentatively. She set about fixing her coffee the way she liked it, waiting for a response from Stephanie. Her unease was palpable, and she struggled not to squirm in her seat.

"It's fine, I'm glad you were able to have a few hours of peace."

She watched as Stephanie sipped her own coffee, but still avoided eye contact. She wanted to press her further, to make sure that she was okay, but she knew she was never one to talk about her feelings. Stephanie may think she didn't have the capacity to feel, but Meredith knew better, and one day soon they would have to talk about this.

"So, have you heard from Kathleen recently?"

The non-sequitur threw Meredith for a moment, that was the last thing she expected to be asked. She had supposed Kathleen would come up at some point during Stephanie's visit, just not right this minute. She took a bite of toast to delay answering while she gathered her thoughts.

"She's texted me a few times over the last few weeks, but I've only given her a general 'yes, I'm okay' reply."

"What do you think you will do? I mean, you still love each other, right?"

Meredith looked at Stephanie properly for the first time that morning. She looked uncomfortable, fidgeting in her chair, and still avoiding eye contact. Meredith was an intelligent woman, and she liked to think she was a good judge of character and right now, she knew Stephanie was hiding something, or at the very least searching for information. She was acting differently from the way she always had in the past. Even when they were captured together her face was always open and engaging. The way she sat here now, nervous and clearly anxious, prickled Meredith's senses.

"I'm not really sure how to answer that. Yes, I do love her, but I don't think I'm in love with her anymore. Moreover, I'm not sure I ever was, not fully."

Meredith was transfixed by the sudden change of Stephanie's demeanour. In an instant, her body calmed and all the tension that was radiating off her a moment ago was absent. And for the first time that day, she looked at Meredith with eyes bright and a wide smile firmly in place.

"Steph, I'm not sure what's going on with me at the moment, but what I do know is I'm not ready for any kind of relationship right now. I don't want anybody to get hurt." Meredith couldn't explain her reaction to Stephanie. She had the worrying sensation she was attracted to her; however, even if she was, she was not in the position to act on those feelings. It was true what she said, she didn't want to hurt anybody, especially Stephanie. She needed to sort things out with Kathleen and figure out her growing attraction to Stephanie.

"I just want you to be happy, Meredith. I can't believe she would be with somebody else and hurt you like that after what you went through." Stephanie stood and took her mug and plate to the sink. She turned around and leaned back against the worktop, stuffing her hands into her jeans pocket and flicking her hair out of her eyes.

Meredith couldn't help but think how attractive she was standing there, tall and lean with a good amount of sexiness.

"It's hard for me to explain how I feel," Stephanie continued. "All I know is I would do anything to take your pain away. It kills me to think what he did to you and for Kathleen to be so selfish. It's unbearable."

Meredith could see the anguish in her face and it warmed her to know how much she was cared for, but also, she hated how much her own problems upset Stephanie.

"Everything is going to be fine," Meredith said as she stood from the table. She took her own things to the sink and then regarded Stephanie. "I'm going to be okay. I will keep seeing my counsellor and I will work things through with Kathleen. Please don't worry about me."

"I can't help it, Mare. I care about you. I don't want you to hurt anymore."

Meredith was at a loss. Never had anyone looked at her with so much adoration and deep longing. It was clear in her eyes how much she cared. Meredith was overcome with worry they each might be feeling an attraction toward the other that at best was unhealthy. She knew to form attachments to people in dire circumstances could happen and she feared this was happening now. She knew this, but still she did not stop herself from pulling Stephanie into her and hugging her tightly.

"Thank you," she whispered.

They moved back from each and Stephanie searched her eyes, looking for something Meredith didn't think she knew how to give anymore. She stepped back and cleared her throat.

"When you're ready, I would really like to show you around Bristol."

"Yes, I would enjoy that. Let me just go clean myself up and I'll be ready."

Meredith escaped to her own room, lost in her thoughts. They were heading for trouble, she knew, but she could not control this any more than she could control the earth's rotation. She grabbed her rain mac from her wardrobe, glad summer was arriving, but wanting to be prepared in case it got too cold or rained and went to see what the day would bring.

†

"Did you say you wanted mushrooms?" Meredith asked Stephanie whilst covering the receiver with her hand.

"Please, if that's okay?"

Meredith relayed the order into the phone for the pizza parlour and then replaced it back on its stand. She settled on the couch at the opposite end from Stephanie and watched her sip her beer. They had enjoyed a nice day together and most of the tension from this morning was absent. Meredith was glad for that, she enjoyed her time with Stephanie and she didn't want it marred by unanswerable questions.

Stephanie glanced at her and smiled, and she couldn't help but smile back.

"Thank you, for today," Stephanie said. "I enjoyed meeting Larry, he seems like a nice guy."

Meredith had intended just to pop into the office to check everything was okay since she hadn't been there for a few days. Larry had been working overtime and his presence surprised Meredith. She quickly recovered and introduced Stephanie as a friend and ushered her out of the office, not wanting to go into details.

"I'm glad you had a nice time. I'm sorry you couldn't see the new shopping centre, but I really don't think I could have handled all those people too well."

Stephanie reached out and gently took her hand. "Please don't apologise. You have only been home a few weeks and you have made brilliant progress. Please don't worry."

Meredith was about to reply, but a key turning the lock in the front door interrupted her. She stood from the couch just as Kathleen came through the entryway. Meredith rushed around the couch, intercepting her before she came fully into the room.

"What are you doing here?" she asked aggressively. She watched as Kathleen's gaze tracked around the room and landed on Stephanie, confusion soon giving way to recognition.

"What is going on? Why is she here?"

"That is none of your business. I ask again, why are you here?"

"I wanted to check on you because you haven't been answering my texts."

"I have answered them, just not in the way I would normally." She raked her hand through her hair, pissed off at the interruption to her evening. "And besides, in case you have forgotten, you slept with someone else and I told you I needed time."

"For God's sake, Meredith! Can you really blame me for wanting to escape for a while? Every time I look at you my head is filled with images of what he did. I don't think I can cope with seeing those visions every day."

Meredith's worst fears had just been vocalised by Kathleen. She knew her scars would be a turn-off for a lot of people, and she wouldn't expect a new partner to be comfortable with them, but for her long-term partner to say these things was heart-breaking.

"What the hell is wrong with you?" Stephanie asked. Meredith hadn't heard her move from the couch to stand behind her. "Meredith has just survived eight months of the worst hell imaginable and all you can think about is how she looks? She is a beautiful person, on the inside, not just the outside, and the fact that she has a few scars shouldn't detract from that beauty."

"This has nothing to do with you," Kathleen seethed. "This is a private conversation between me and my partner."

Meredith had heard enough, and she did not want an argument kicking off in her apartment. She turned to Stephanie. "Can you go wait in the kitchen, please?" She didn't miss the look of hurt that flashed across her face. After Stephanie left, she turned back to Kathleen.

"Kath, I can't do this anymore. We're over. And if you ask yourself honestly you will agree it was over before I was even taken."

Kathleen sagged against the wall behind her and briefly closed her eyes. "I know, you're right. But I don't want you to hate me. I wish we could have worked things out, but I can't deal with this, not now."

Meredith struggled to contain the tears that were forming. Yes, she had known it was over between them for months, however, actually admitting that and following through with it was a whole different matter. She stepped forward and gave Kathleen a hug.

"I'm sorry. I suppose I should ask for my key back."

Kathleen complied and, after handing it over, Meredith closed the door behind her and went in search of Stephanie. She found her pacing in a small circle in the kitchen, and Meredith couldn't miss the anger that was coursing through her body. The tension was vibrating off her in waves and Meredith wanted to do anything she could to calm her.

"Stephanie?"

Stephanie glanced at her, but quickly looked away, continuing to wear a path in the floorboards. Meredith was dismayed to feel tears falling down her cheeks as she walked over to her.

"Steph, please."

Stephanie stopped her pacing, and properly looking at her before Meredith could say any more Stephanie swept her up in a tight embrace.

"I'm sorry," she whispered into Meredith's hair. "I shouldn't have butted in, but I couldn't just sit there anymore and allow her to say those horrible things to you."

"Thank you for standing up for me. You have no idea what it means to me to have you on my side."

"Always."

Meredith gazed up into Stephanie's warm green eyes, and it was impossible not to notice the longing that was in them. She raised her hand and gently placed it onto Stephanie's cheek, marvelling at her soft skin.

"What's happening here?"

Stephanie leaned into her touch and said, "I'm not sure, all I know is I don't want to go home tomorrow."

"Do you think maybe this is some kind of attachment disorder that has happened between us because of that place?"

"Possibly, but does it really matter? Can't we just continue the way we are?"

"Of course, it matters. The last thing we both need is for something to happen between us and then for it to turn out to be false. I don't want to hurt you any more than you have been in your life, and I'm worried that's what will happen." Meredith moved away from her and went to the sink, gazing out the window but not really seeing anything. "Why is it you think you are the only one I can bear touching me? Just being near you makes me feel safe."

"Perhaps it's because we were there together," Stephanie said as she came to stand behind her, close but not touching.

Meredith shook her head. "No, I don't think that's it." She turned around and searched her face. "You are a very special woman, Stephanie." Without giving it a thought Meredith moved closer. She raised onto her tiptoes, gently kissing Stephanie on the lips. It was a quick kiss, only a couple of seconds long, however, it shook something loose in Meredith and she started to cry. Stephanie's arms came around her, holding her close.

"It's okay, Mare, we'll figure this out together."

Meredith hoped she was right, that they could work through this. She didn't know how this would end or what she wanted, all she knew was being in Stephanie's arms felt right. She felt safe and protected and she never wanted to let go.

†

Stephanie threw down her uneaten piece of pizza crust into the box that sat on the coffee table. Leaning back with a groan, she said, "I'm stuffed, that was delicious." It had taken a while for her appetite to come back after being starved for so long, and she struggled to finish most meals. Meredith sat beside her, nursing a glass of Cabernet Sauvignon, staring off into space. Stephanie regarded her quiet companion. They hadn't really spoken much since the scene in the kitchen. Not long after that the pizza had arrived, and they set about collecting wine glasses, cutlery, and napkins. She could understand Meredith's sombre mood, this was a confusing time for her as well. Being with Meredith felt right. She had enjoyed their day together and loved getting to know the place her friend called home. It had been a pleasant day until Kathleen had arrived. She was just as beautiful as Stephanie remembered and just as dismissive of Stephanie's presence. She could not miss the look of revulsion on her face as Kathleen looked at Stephanie. But that was fine with Stephanie, she did not much like the woman herself. The way she had been treating Meredith since her return was abhorrent. Just because her partner may have changed physically did not mean she wasn't the same person. Sure, Meredith had some emotional repercussions from her time in captivity, but she didn't deserve to be cheated on. And to come to Meredith's door and literally say she couldn't even look at her was disgusting.

Stephanie could feel her anger bubbling up again the same way it had earlier. Meredith was such a sweet person and Stephanie could see how much she cared about people just from the glint in her eye when she spoke of her family and friends. Stephanie had no choice but to stand up to Kathleen, and if not for Meredith intercepting her, she gladly would have punched Kathleen in the face. Stephanie was not a violent person, but the woman deserved a good thump.

Meredith's hand moved onto her thigh and gently rubbed back and forth. It was a soothing touch and it helped still her frustration.

"What's the matter, Stephanie? I can feel your anger from here."

She blinked a few times to clear her mind from the memories of earlier that evening. She considered Meredith's compassionate eyes and she found herself speaking without reservation.

"How can anybody look at you and not see how wonderful you are? The things we went through there would be enough to destroy even the strongest of people, but we made it out. You were there for so long Meredith..." Her voice trailed off as she closed her eyes, trying to stop the tears that were forming. She shook her head. "You're amazing. When I am with you, I feel things I never knew I could. You'd have to be a pretty special person for that to happen to me. It never has before."

Meredith delicately placed a hand on her cheek. Her fingers were so soft on her skin and she never wanted her to move.

"Oh, honey. How is it possible you are still single? You went through some bad stuff too, and you're sitting here telling me how strong I am? You are the strong one, you're the one supporting me when I so clearly have struggled to readjust."

"If I am strong it is because of you. You make me feel brave." There was no doubt in Stephanie's mind that she was attracted to Meredith. Every conversation, every email brought Meredith closer, and it wasn't something she wanted to fight anymore. She knew Meredith was in a bad place, knew she would not be ready for anything to happen between them. Hell, she didn't even know if Meredith felt the same, so she would wait, she would wait forever for Meredith.

"I need time, Steph," Meredith said as if reading her mind. "Baby steps."

"Baby steps," Stephanie repeated.

Meredith moved away and stood. She gave herself a shake and began clearing away the detritus from the meal.

"Here, let me help."

"No, stay put. I'll do it."

Stephanie closed her eyes and thought back to the other part of the evening, which had scared and thrilled her at the same time. When Meredith had unexpectedly kissed her on the lips, she had gone numb. She had no other words to describe it, just complete numbness. The taste of those sweet lips had paralysed her. She had never felt anything so totally out of this world and right in her life. Holding Meredith in her arms while she cried was the most painful thing in the world for Stephanie to endure. She hated to see the pain and knowing it was Meredith's feelings for her that caused that pain tore her up.

Meredith came back into the lounge and Stephanie looked to where she stood with a hip resting against the arm of the chair. Meredith was gazing at her with an unreadable expression as if trying to figure out something which she had no answers for. Her eyes roamed from Stephanie's face, down her body, and back up. Heat shot up Stephanie's body and she gave a little gasp as the intensity of Meredith's gaze ignited her flesh, sending goose bumps all over her skin. She doubted Meredith was intentionally trying to turn her on, but she had. She had never felt such arousal before and she looked away for fear of her own reactions alerting Meredith to the direction Stephanie's thoughts had gone.

"Sweet Jesus," Meredith whispered.

Stephanie mentally rolled her eyes. She was obviously not doing a very good job of hiding her feelings. After all the years of worrying she had no feelings at all, suddenly her feelings were telegraphed to the world

"I'm going to have a shower," Meredith said, breaking the connection between them.

"Sure, okay." Stephanie stood, stuffing her hands into her jeans pocket, her body tense. She held her breath as Meredith slowly walked toward her, not stopping until she was inches from her body. She looked up into Stephanie's eyes and Stephanie could see the indecision there. She did nothing, just held her gaze, letting Meredith examine her, finding the answers she wanted.

"When do you have to leave tomorrow?" Meredith asked.

Stephanie let out her breath in a whoosh. "There's a train at eleven or three."

"Okay. If I take you to the station, we have until two thirty to do something."

"Yes."

"Okay. I'm going to go take that shower now." Meredith nodded and took a step back from her, longing still in her eyes. Two more steps back, then she turned and hurried to the bathroom.

Stephanie ran a hand through her hair. "Shit." Things were becoming intense between them. They needed to get this under control. It was too soon after the West incident, and they still had the court case to deal with. She doubted Meredith was fully aware of what she was doing. Hell, even she didn't know what was happening between them, only that she wanted it to continue.

She went into her own room and readied herself for bed. The next conscious thought she had was the feeling of the bed dipping and Meredith's warm body scooting in next to hers. Stephanie automatically opened her arms for her and cuddled her close.

"I hope this okay," Meredith whispered.

Stephanie didn't reply. She kissed her forehead and pulled her closer. She knew deep down they were heading for a giant mess, but she didn't care. Being here with Meredith like this felt too right, too perfect. She closed her eyes, let out a breath, and slept.

†

Meredith pulled her car into one of the few spaces left at the train station at the drop-off point. She switched off the engine, but neither woman made a move to exit the car. Stephanie looked out the window at the people milling about. For a Sunday, the station was busy. She turned and smiled shyly at Meredith.

"I want to thank you for having me, but that just doesn't seem like enough."

Meredith blew out a breath and laced her fingers with Stephanie's.

"Thank you for coming down. It has been a weekend of learning new things."

Stephanie caught her eye and their gazes locked. She really did not want to leave. The thought of going back to York, and carrying on with her life without seeing Meredith, was not something she relished.

"I hope I haven't made you uncomfortable this weekend. I didn't plan for any of this." She saw the blush work its way up Meredith's smooth skin and she smiled, thinking back to that morning. Stephanie had awakened in her arms and her thigh was wedged tightly between Meredith's own limbs. She was aware of her laboured breathing and she could feel the heat between Meredith's legs. She had looked up into her eyes and could see the arousal in them; however, more importantly, she could see the fear that was so plainly written on her face. Stephanie quickly moved away mumbling apologies, but Meredith had stopped her with a hand on her wrist. She whispered it was okay, just a shock.

Stephanie didn't believe her. She knew how difficult it would be for Meredith to accept any kind of sexual yearnings for somebody after what happened with Jameson West. She herself was confused by it. Somebody like Meredith, with her kind and caring nature, would undoubtedly have mixed feelings toward this reaction. Meredith needed time, and Stephanie would give that to her. She would not rush her. They both had things they needed to work through, and hopefully Meredith would not run away from this. After so many years of being alone, Stephanie had finally found somebody who brightened her world, made her feel excited for life, and she was not going to give that up willingly.

Meredith's kiss on her cheek brought her back to the present. Stephanie's hand involuntarily went to the place her lips had touched as she shook her head, mesmerised.

"Will you let me know when you arrive home?" Meredith asked.

"Of course. It may not be until late."

"I don't care what time of the night it is, you make sure you ring me."

The panic in her voice did not go unnoticed by Stephanie. She gently cradled Meredith's chin in her hand.

"I promise you, I will call you. Nothing will happen to me." Her eyes bored into Meredith's trying to make her believe that everything would be fine. She could see the worry in her face. After all, it was in York that they had both gone missing. "He's in prison, Meredith, he cannot hurt us anymore."

"I know, you're right. I just worry." The tension in Meredith's body seemed to release as she sat back into her seat. She blew out a breath.

"Perfectly understandable. I'll be careful."

Meredith looked at her and smiled sweetly. "I'm going to miss you. You will keep in contact, won't you?"

"Every day."

Meredith searched her face and Stephanie was pleased that she seemed to find what she was looking for. She couldn't go without feeling those lips again. The memory of the taste of them had been teasing her since the day before, and she knew she would not settle until she tasted them again. She moved forward slowly, giving Meredith enough time to move if she wanted to if a kiss wasn't welcome. To her delight, Meredith didn't move away, just tilted her head and slid her eyes closed.

Stephanie didn't touch anywhere else, she kept her hands to herself, not wanting to freak Meredith out. She gently placed her lips on Meredith's and left them there. She made no attempt to deepen the kiss any more than what it was. A kiss of goodbye, thank you, and a promise to see you soon. She moved back and watched transfixed as Meredith opened her eyes, now darkened to deep indigo blue.

"Wow." Meredith touched her own lips with her fingertips, the shock evident on her face. "I think you should go now, Steph."

She didn't answer but hefted her bag out from the back seat and grabbed the handle of the door. She yanked it open with more force than necessary, desperate to get out of the car before she decided to stay and never go home. If she didn't leave now, she never would.

She ducked back and made eye contact with Meredith, who still sat with a hand to her mouth, eyes wide. "Thanks again. Speak to you soon." Without waiting for a reply, she slung her bag on her back and quickly walked into the station entrance. She did not look back for fear that if she saw Meredith her resolve would disappear, and she would stay. All the unfamiliar thoughts and emotions jumbled up inside her, scaring her, and she struggled for air. She had never felt so much all at once before, and it terrified her to know she had no idea what she was doing.

She thumbed through the contacts on her mobile phone while waiting in line for her ticket and shot off a quick text to Fiona asking to meet with her as soon as possible. She needed to talk this through with someone and nobody knew her better than Joe's wife.

CHAPTER FIFTEEN

"Meredith? What are you doing here?" Carrie asked as she opened her door.

"I know I should have called, but I came here straight from the train station. I've just dropped off Stephanie and I don't know what to do." Meredith was dismayed to feel tears brimming in her eyes and she had no choice but to let them roll down her cheeks.

"Jesus Christ." Carrie grabbed hold of her hand and quickly pulled her through the foyer and straight into the lounge. She was quickly gathered into a hug. "What's the matter, honey?"

Meredith pulled back from Carrie, shaking her head. She gazed around Carrie's new home, thinking the more intimate decor and furnishings suited Holly and Carrie's new life together. She only knew them together, as a couple. Meredith had met with Carrie to discuss a new business property and house after she had left her job and was ready to set up on her own. She had met Holly a few weeks later when the two had got back together after being separated for a while, and Meredith thought them a wonderful couple.

"I'm not sure where to start." She turned back to Carrie, whose face was creased with worry. She blew out a breath and pinched the bridge of her nose, trying to get her thoughts in order. Carrie led her to the sofa and made her sit.

"I'm going to make some coffee."

While Meredith sat on her own in the living room, she tried to get her head around the feelings she was having for Stephanie. She wasn't sure what to do about them. Stephanie was a beautiful, handsome woman, with her strong jaw and captivating eyes, and Meredith loved to just look at her. She was attracted to Stephanie, sexually, and that was the thought that was scaring her the most. She didn't know how to handle this new development. After all, she had spent eight months being brutalised, her girlfriend had cheated on her, and now she had these new feelings for Stephanie. She hadn't thought she would have these thoughts and urges ever again considering what she had been through, but just looking at Stephanie made her pulse race. This weekend was the first time they had seen each other since the hospital and Meredith was shocked at how much she already missed her. They had grown close with the emails they had sent back and forth over the last few weeks and seeing her this weekend solidified to her how much she enjoyed Stephanie's company. She had her reservations, though. She wondered if her attraction stemmed from their time in captivity.

Before Meredith's thoughts could travel any further in that direction, Carrie came back into the room carrying two steaming mugs of coffee. She placed one in front of Meredith on the small glass coffee table and took a seat next to her.

"So, what is going on?" Carrie asked as she settled into the loveseat.

Meredith took a deep breath and said, "I have feelings for Stephanie."

Carrie didn't reply. She just sat there blinking rapidly, absorbing the statement.

"Also, Kathleen came by last night and we broke up."

"Wow."

"I'm not sure what is happening. With everything that is going on I didn't think I could have these kinds of feelings with anyone. That's why I didn't mind Kathleen cheating on me. Of course, I was upset that she did, but I was not overly worried by it. I was more concerned that she found me lacking somehow."

"Mare, if there's one thing I know for sure, it is that you are a strong, beautiful woman, and nothing that guy did will ever take that away from you. Kathleen is the one with the problem, not you."

"Thank you. It's okay, the way Stephanie looks at me makes me believe what you are saying is true." Meredith reached out her hand and briefly touched Carrie on her shoulder.

"So, she feels the same?" Carrie asked and then took a sip of coffee.

"Yes. When she looks at me, I can see how much she cares for me. She has the sweetest lips, they feel so right touching mine."

Carrie sputtered the coffee she had just taken a sip of back into her mug and went into a coughing fit.

"There has been kissing?" she asked between gasps.

"Oh, not really, just a couple of pecks whilst we've hugged. She makes me feel so safe, especially through the night—"

"You've spent the night together?"

Meredith blushed, and she could feel the heat creeping up her neck and settling on her cheeks. She recalled the two nights that she had slept peacefully in Stephanie's arms, feeling protected and loved. She had not spent a peaceful night like that since she had been home.

"Not like that. I had a nightmare the first night she was there and she comforted me. The second night, I just needed to be close to her after what had happened with Kathleen. She is a really special woman, Carrie."

Carrie studied her for a few moments and Meredith could see her trying to comprehend all of this. Her forehead creased as she drew her eyebrows together, her lips pursed.

"I'm going to guess that you are struggling with this new development."

"Yes. You know how I struggle with people touching me? I still flinch if people are too close, but with her, it's like the barriers are gone. When she holds me it just feels right, like we are connected on a deeper level, but I can't help wondering if the connection I feel with her is a product of our kidnapping. I'm worried this is a false emotion and we have just latched onto each other."

"What does Stephanie think?"

Meredith put her now empty mug on the table and crossed her legs under herself. She ran her fingers through her hair, scratching her scalp. "She thinks we should go slow,

130

carry on getting to know each other. She doesn't appear to be overly concerned about the way we met, she's just happy that we did."

"Perhaps she's right. You both live quite a distance away from each other so it's not like you'll be seeing a lot of one another. Keep talking over the phone and email and see where it leads. You might find over time that you have nothing in common and run out of things to say. If this is because of the kidnapping, it'll fizzle out once you are both in a better place."

"You're probably right. I am rather worried about her, though." At Carrie's raised eyebrow, she continued. "Stephanie appears to have already moved on from the kidnapping and doesn't relate her time there the same as mine. She gets angry when we talk about what he did to me but shows no emotion if we talk about her experience."

"You think maybe she's suppressing it? Pretending it didn't happen?"

"I'm not sure. She was in an accident as a small child, which, she thinks, stole her ability to have feelings or emotions about things. She can be empathetic to others at certain times, but she never feels anything for herself. Does that make sense?"

Meredith shook her head at her inability to explain the problems Stephanie had. Stephanie was adamant that it was due to the accident, but Meredith was sure it was the loss of her mother that led her to hide her feelings and not wanting to risk being hurt again.

"I think I'll mention it to my counsellor at my next meeting, see if she has PTSD or something."

Carrie glanced at her watch. "Holly should be back from the graveyard soon. Do you want to go out for a bite to eat?"

Holly's sister had died the year before and Holly visited her grave often, still missing the only blood family she had left. Meredith did not want to think about surviving that kind of loss, how devastating that must be. Her mind flashed to Stephanie. She had no family of her own either. If not for her good friend Joe, Meredith wondered who Stephanie would have become.

She realised she had zoned out for a moment when Carrie cleared her throat and nudged her with her sock-covered foot.

"Oh, sorry. Yes, that would be nice. Somewhere not too crowded, though. I still get a little panicky if there are too many people about."

"No problem, I know just the place."

†

Stephanie sat comfortably on the plush pink leather sofa in Fiona's lounge while Fiona sat opposite her on a footstool. They both cradled a tumbler containing two fingers of whiskey. After Stephanie had arrived home from Meredith's three days ago, she had spent that time working and sleeping, not wanting to visit her growing attraction toward Meredith. She knew in her heart that she had developed strong feelings for Meredith, but she didn't want to entertain the idea that this attachment might be because of the ordeal they both shared.

Stephanie knew she had to talk to somebody and Fiona was that somebody. She supposed maybe she could talk to Joe; however, he would most likely say what she didn't want to hear, that Meredith was right, that her feelings were due to the kidnapping. He was her best friend, but sometimes she just needed a woman's perspective and there was no opinion she respected more than Fiona's.

She had arrived over an hour ago, but she had yet to broach the subject of why she was really here. They had chatted vaguely about her visit to Meredith's, but Stephanie had skimmed over the most important details. Fiona wasn't stupid. Stephanie could see by the crease above her eyebrows and her pursed lips that Fiona knew something was going on.

"I'm not sure what to do. We had a really nice time together and we grew closer, closer than I've ever been with anybody. I've told her things that even Joe doesn't know, and I'm scared of what this could mean." Stephanie took another gulp of the whiskey, enjoying the burn as it slid down her throat. "I've never felt like this before with anyone. She is so beautiful and strong-willed, I just want to protect her and make her safe."

Fiona stared at her unblinkingly. Finally, she took a deep breath, blinked, and shook her head. "I know you guys went through a lot together and you definitely formed a bond, but you can't base a relationship on those things alone. You need to ask yourself if the kidnapping hadn't happened, and you met randomly in a bar, say, would you still be attracted to her? Do you find her sexually attractive?"

Stephanie didn't even ponder the questions, she answered instantly. "Yes." She ran her fingers through her hair, a soft smile overtaking her lips. She thought about the weekend she had spent with Meredith and all the things they had talked about. The kidnapping was hardly discussed. They had spent the time having fun and getting to know each other. She knew without a doubt her feelings for Meredith were real.

"I think what happened to us probably did bond us together, but everything that happened after that, and the way she makes me feel, proves to me my feelings are real."

Fiona was about to respond when Joe walked in. Stephanie looked at him standing in the doorway of the lounge and was dismayed by the look of disgust on his face. She could tell he was angry, his face getting redder by the second. She had never seen him like this before. For the first time since she had known him she feared him. She didn't scare easily but seeing him like this terrified her.

"Did I just hear right?" Joe asked through gritted teeth, his voice unnaturally quiet for him. "You think you honestly have feelings for her?" He stepped farther into the room and Stephanie stood. They ended up face-to-face, only inches separating them. "I get why you might think this is true, but this is all just in your head. There is no way you feel anything for her except pity."

Stephanie flinched at the last word, her own anger growing. She closed the distance between them and shoved Joe as hard as she could, sending him backwards flat on his ass. Before he had a chance to stand, she stood over him.

"Don't you say another fucking word about her! You don't know her or what we went through together. You're supposed to be my fucking friend and support me. This is no longer up for discussion. I'm falling for her and I want to see where this goes, understand?" She stepped back from him and turned to face Fiona, who still sat in her chair, shock clearly displayed on her face. "Sorry about this, I guess I'll be leaving now." She leaned over to collect her phone and keys from the end table.

"You're making a mistake," Joe said from directly behind her. She hadn't heard him get up. She kept her back to him and didn't respond. He continued. "Are you that desperate to find someone you'd take on any hopeless case?"

She couldn't believe what he had just said. They had been friends for the last five years and this was the first time he had ever said anything so nasty to her. She didn't think, she clenched her fist, and in one quick motion, turned and punched him in the face. The crack of his nose was unmistakable as blood spilled out over the carpet.

Fiona shot to her feet and rushed to her husband's side. Joe had his head cradled in his hands. She turned to Stephanie and in a calm voice said, "You need to leave, now."

Stephanie shook out her fist, her knuckles burning with pain. She wouldn't be surprised if she had broken something. She'd never been one for fist fights. Yes, she had her fair share of scuffles in the past, but she had never punched anyone like she had Joe. He was her best friend, and they had never had a falling out like this before, but she refused to apologise. She would never let anyone talk about Meredith the way he had. Regardless of whether Stephanie had feelings for her or not, what he said was disgusting.

She grabbed her things and went to the front door. Before she could open it, she felt Fiona's hand on her shoulder turning her around. She expected Fiona to be angry, furious, with her and was shocked by the kindness and sympathy in her face. She was dismayed to feel tears stinging her eyes.

"I…"

Fiona cupped her cheeks in her warm hands, and brought her head down, kissing her on her forehead.

"Steph, it's okay. He was out of line, but he's worried about you. He just wants to protect you."

"I know, and I am sorry, but I can't deal with his negativity right now. Why can't he just support me in this?"

"He just doesn't want you getting hurt again. He loves you."

Stephanie blew out a breath and Fiona released her. She supposed she should say sorry to Joe, for the sake of their friendship, but it would have to wait. She was too keyed up and angry to face him. She pulled Fiona into a tight hug and kissed her on the cheek.

"I love him too, and you. I don't know what I would do without you both. I'll speak to him in a few days once we have both calmed down." Stephanie opened the door behind her, walked to the rental car she had hired yesterday, got in, and left.

It was coming up to eleven o'clock by the time she got home. She wanted to speak to Meredith, but it was too late at night. It would have to wait until tomorrow.

†

Meredith settled on her couch, swinging her legs up to occupy the full length of the two-seater. She grabbed her laptop off the floor, and after waiting for it to boot up, she connected to Skype. She clicked onto Stephanie's handle and waited for her to answer. They hadn't spoken at all yesterday and she felt something was wrong. They didn't go a day without any form of contact between them, even if it was just a text message. Meredith had left a voicemail for her yesterday morning, but as of yet, Stephanie hadn't replied. Before she had a chance for her worries to spiral out of control, Stephanie answered.

"Meredith? What time is it?"

Stephanie's image filled her screen and Meredith was shocked by what she saw. Stephanie had dark circles under her eyes and her normally gorgeous hair was lacklustre. Her skin was pale and her vibrant eyes dull.

"It's about half two in the afternoon. Are you just getting up now?"

"Yes, I kind of had a rough night."

Stephanie lifted her right hand and scrubbed it over her face, obviously in a vain effort to try and rouse herself. As she did this, Meredith couldn't contain the gasp that came from her lips. She could clearly see Stephanie's hand was heavily bruised and swollen.

"What the hell happened to your hand?"

Stephanie glanced down at the hand in question and shrugged her shoulders. "It's nothing, I banged it up at work."

"Don't lie to me. In the few months I've known you, you have never once lied to me. Please don't start now."

Meredith could see the indecision. Something big must have happened for Stephanie not to trust her. After all the conversations they had shared, Meredith was certain Stephanie would always be honest with her.

"Really, it's no big deal. I kind of got into a scuffle with Joe and I ended up breaking his nose."

"What on earth could have happened for you two to get in a fight? He's like your brother."

Stephanie's face disappeared from her screen for a few seconds as she got out of bed. She came back into view when she sat on her small couch.

"Honestly, everything is fine. He said a few things I didn't like, and I hit him. End of."

"But you two have never had a falling out like that before. What the hell did he say to make you go off like that?"

Stephanie didn't reply. Meredith came to the only conclusion that she could think of. She knew about Joe's reservations regarding her and Stephanie becoming friends, and that could be the only thing that would have brought about trouble in their relationship.

"This is because of me, isn't it?"

Stephanie took a deep breath and looked away from her phone. She whispered, "Yes."

"Tell me what he said."

"Look, you don't need to know the details. This is between me and Joe. I'll give him a call at some point and apologise and everything will be fine."

Meredith set her laptop onto her coffee table and stood. She paced the living room, trying to calm herself. Her pulse quickened as she thought of all the things Joe could possibly have said to make Stephanie snap. She could hear Stephanie's voice coming from her laptop, calling her name. She sat back onto the couch.

"I ask again, what did he say? I deserve to know."

After waiting a few seconds Stephanie finally answered. "He just said the same things he's been saying all along, that becoming friends isn't a good idea for all the reasons that you already know."

"It has to be more than that, tell me."

"Basically, he said that my feelings aren't real, that I just pity you. He also said I was desperate and would take on any hopeless case."

A few tears escaped Meredith's eyes, rolling down her cheeks. She wiped them away angrily, refusing to give in to the hopelessness that was creeping back into her world.

"Meredith, please don't cry. It kills me to see you crying. It's not worth getting upset over. You've got enough on your plate without worrying about this. What he said isn't true. You know I don't think that way about you."

"You know what? The reason I rang you today is that I think we need to talk."

Meredith knew she was making a mistake with what she was about to do, but Stephanie had very limited people in her life, and Joe and his wife were her family. She needed to do this, no matter how much it would hurt.

"I've been thinking over the last few days, since you left here, that maybe we should take a break. We haven't really had a chance to settle back into our own lives and I think everybody is right, seeing you and talking to you keeps bringing up everything that happened." Even though Stephanie began crying, Meredith continued, "I think it's for the best. I'm planning on going back to work in a week or two, full-time, and the court case is coming up. I need to make sure I'm strong for that. You need to work things out with Joe, he's your family."

She could see Stephanie shaking, and if it was possible, she turned even paler. This was the last thing Meredith wanted to do. Being with Stephanie the previous weekend, and all the times they had spoken, solidified in her mind that she wanted a relationship with Stephanie, or at least try to see if they could build one. But there was no way on earth she would allow Stephanie to lose the only people she cared about. And more, Meredith had been through a terrible ordeal and she felt hesitant about allowing someone into her life who would be capable of such violence, even if it was in defence of her. She needed to protect herself. She needed to keep her walls erected and not allow anyone to hurt her again. If Stephanie was capable of hitting her best friend, what would she do if she got angry with Meredith?

"Don't do this," Stephanie pleaded. "You don't mean that. Please? Just take it back."

"I'm sorry, Stephanie. I have to do what's best for me and being around you isn't it."

Without giving her a chance to reply, Meredith shut the lid of the laptop with more force than she intended. She bent over and cradled her waist, head on her knees, and wept. She thought she had experienced excruciating pain before, locked up in that hellhole. But seeing the look of anguish in Stephanie's eyes was unbearable. Meredith had intentionally hurt the one person who had ever made her feel safe.

CHAPTER SIXTEEN

It was close to eight thirty at night and Meredith was already on her third glass of wine. After she had finally calmed down, she ran a hot bath and attempted to block out the constant ringing of her phone and the beeping of her Skype alerts. In the end, she couldn't bear the noise any longer, and after drying her body off, she turned off her phone and shut down her laptop. She attempted to eat a sandwich but couldn't even swallow the first bite. She decided wine would be easier to stomach.

As she reached for the bottle to top off her glass a sudden loud pounding came from her front door. She stood from the sofa and put on her silk robe. The pounding came again.

"Meredith? Meredith, open the door."

The voice stopped her in her tracks. She ran her fingers through her hair and tried to calm the rising panic that was bubbling up within her. Her palms were sweating, her heart rate rising. She couldn't shake the fear Stephanie might hurt her. She reached for the door handle but didn't open it.

"What are you doing here, Steph?"

"Please let me in, I need to see you."

She could hear the panic and heartbreak and she refused to hurt Stephanie any more. Against her better judgement, she opened the door. What she saw terrified her. Stephanie's eyes were wide with grief, the skin around them puffy. The desperation in her face was not hard to miss.

Before she could say anything, Stephanie stormed passed her straight into the living room. Meredith closed the door and followed her in.

"I left the minute your phone was switched off when I called and drove like a mad woman trying to get here. Why didn't you answer your phone? I thought something had happened to you, that you might have done something stupid."

"I told you we needed to take a break. That doesn't mean I'm suicidal."

"I know, I know. But I needed to speak with you, and when I couldn't get hold of you my mind went into overdrive. You can't just tell me that you don't want to see me anymore just because of some stupid words that Joe said. That's not fair to you or me. You know there's something between us, you know you have feelings for me the same as I have feelings for you."

Meredith sat down in her previous position and picked up her glass. She took a long swallow, then set the glass back on the table.

"Yes, I do have feelings for you and that's why I did this. He's your family and you need him. Not only that, I was worried for my safety. You scared me, Steph, knowing you could hit Joe."

Stephanie sat beside her on the sofa and tentatively took her hand.

"Families are supposed to support each other, and even if they disagree with your decisions they should never be as cruel and disgusting as Joe was. I won't have someone talking about you like that, you don't deserve it." She raised her other hand, the swelling in her fingers still clearly visible, and placed it on Meredith's cheek, gently caressing the scar there. "And I also won't allow you to push me away. You're the first person to ever make me feel anything and I can't let you go. Please, Meredith, don't push me away. I didn't mean to scare you. I promise you, I would never lay a finger on you. I have never hit anyone in my entire life. I just couldn't stop myself when he said those horrible things about you."

Meredith's heart broke at the vulnerability in Stephanie's eyes. She relaxed her stiff body and let out a sigh. "Oh, sweetheart, you're so brave. For someone who says she never has any feelings, you're doing a good job of expressing them now. How could I ever let you go? I don't know what's going to happen, but the one thing I'm sure of is I need you in my life. In whatever capacity that may be." Meredith pulled her into a hug and cradled her head whilst Stephanie cried.

"I'm sorry. I'm sorry I ever thought you could hit me. I know how sweet you are. You've always been there for me and I should have known how much you would want to protect me. Forgive me?"

"There's nothing to forgive. I didn't make the best decision hitting Joe and I'm sorry I upset you."

†

Stephanie wasn't sure what had awakened her. She heard a clap of thunder and the rain pelting against the windows was immense. She rubbed her eyes and tried to focus through the dark. She realised she was in Meredith's living room, lying on the sofa with a blanket draped over her. She sat up slowly, and through the darkness, she could see Meredith, leaning against the doorway of her bedroom watching her. She thought now how crazy she must have looked, turning up on her doorstep demanding entry. The last thing she wanted was for Meredith to think she was mad, or worse, a stalker.

"What time is it?"

"It's a little after three o'clock. The storm woke me, and I was on my way to check on you, but somehow I couldn't make my feet move past here."

Stephanie's eyes adjusted to the darkness and she could see the worry in Meredith's eyes. She wasn't sure if Meredith still feared her or was just concerned about her behaviour earlier.

"I'm sorry if I freaked you out today. I didn't mean to come barrelling into your home and upset you."

Meredith rushed toward her and knelt in front of her, grasping her cold hands.

"Oh honey, you haven't scared me, not at all. I'll admit I was fearful for a while when I found out you hit Joe, but after seeing you, talking to you, I know you would never hurt me." She gently rubbed her fingers over Stephanie's injured hand, careful not to put too much pressure on her knuckles. "Did you get this looked at by a doctor?"

"No, I rang the emergency hotline and they said to ice it and keep an eye on it. If the swelling doesn't go down in a few days, then go see my GP." She removed her damaged hand from Meredith's and brushed the soft hair from her face. "What's wrong?"

Meredith took a deep breath and expelled it slowly. Her eyes were shadowed, and Stephanie found them hard to read. She prayed to God she wouldn't be sent away again, just the thought terrified her.

"I'm really concerned for you, Steph. I completely understand you being upset about us not seeing each other anymore, but the way you were earlier, I'm really worried you're not as okay as you say you are. I don't think you've dealt with the loss of your mother or what happened with West, and I'm scared that it's all going to blow up at some point."

Stephanie stood from the sofa and walked toward the lounge window. She opened the blinds and stared through the night at the heavy rain and flashes of lightning that lit up the late spring night. A great many people were frightened of thunderstorms, but Stephanie always found them relaxing, seeing a beauty in them that mystified her. She thought of Meredith's words and she supposed she should be angry with her for trying to tell her how she felt. She wasn't a little child anymore, and she never knew her mum anyway, so how could she have grief about a person she hardly remembered? And West? She was only there a few weeks and she always managed to block out his torture toward her, seeing his abuse as just physical. She had never allowed him to get inside her head. She had been too concerned with trying to get Meredith through it.

"I know what you're thinking," Meredith said from just behind her. "I know what you have told me about not having feelings one way or the other to both events. I think you have become so great at blocking out trauma that you have found a way to cope with feelings you don't want to face. You've got a lot of anger inside you, and if you don't get it sorted, I'm worried about what that could mean for us in the future. I don't want you to keep all this building up inside until one day it blows up and you won't be able to control yourself."

Stephanie's anger got the better of her, after all, that was her go-to emotion when things got difficult.

"How dare you say that." She turned around and faced Meredith. "What, you think just because you've had a few counselling sessions that gives you the right to try and dissect me and tell me how I feel?"

She expected Meredith to get angry, but she didn't. She just took a step forward and pulled Stephanie into a tight embrace. She tried to pull away, but Meredith held her tighter. She thought she had done enough crying today, but apparently not. Slowly tears leaked down her cheeks.

"You said earlier for me not to push you away," Meredith said. "So now I'm asking you to do the same. Don't try and push me away. Let me help you the way you've helped me."

Stephanie lifted her head and gazed into the eyes that were only inches away from her own. "I don't know what you want me to say. I can't tell you about feelings I don't have. I can't stand here and say things have affected me in a way I don't think they have."

"I think they have affected you, you just don't recognise they have. You can get angry at me, shout at me, but all you're doing is confirming what I already expect to be true."

Stephanie pulled away completely and went into the kitchen. She poured herself a glass of water and took a few calming sips. She returned to the living room but didn't approach Meredith, who still stood in the same position. Stephanie looked within herself and began to question everything she believed about herself, every situation she had been in, and her reactions over the years.

She knew she was capable of anger. She knew she could love, she loved Joe and Fiona. She knew empathy for others. And she knew the power of attraction. Her deep need for Meredith was proof of that. Maybe she had been wrong. Maybe the death of her mother did cause her to set up walls, maybe closing herself off all these years had enabled her to never experience that kind of loss or pain again.

She thought of the hopelessness she had felt when Meredith had said she didn't want to see her anymore. How it felt like her heart was being torn out of her chest. It was like her entire life force was being drained out of her veins and she honestly thought she had died inside.

A memory flashed through her mind. She was five years old in a foster home. She could remember sitting at the dining room table with her foster family all around her, and the interaction of the parents to their kids. The mother kissed one of the children's heads as she placed a plate of food in front of him and whispered, "I love you." Stephanie had run from the table and hid in the bathroom, hysterically sobbing on the floor and wondering why nobody loved her like that. She didn't know it at the time, or couldn't remember, that someone did love her like that, her own mother, a mother she would never know.

Stephanie came back to the present and looked up at Meredith.

"Steph? You okay? You're as white as a sheet."

"I just remembered something, something from my childhood. It was the day I realised I would always be alone, I would never have someone love me unconditionally. I think that was the day I shut down emotionally. The day I vowed to never let anybody hurt me the way I was hurting then." She took a few steps toward Meredith, who remained silent as if she knew Stephanie needed to say this. "All these years I thought the head trauma from the accident was the reason I am the way I am, but you're right, I did this to myself."

"Sweetheart, you only did what you thought you had to do. It was the only way you could protect yourself. And that's okay, you needed to be strong, you needed to look after yourself." Meredith closed the distance between them and placed her hands on Stephanie's cheeks. "You don't need to do that anymore. You're not alone and I promise I will never hurt you the way you have been in the past." She pulled Stephanie's head down and kissed her on the lips, remaining there for a few long seconds.

"I'm supposed to be the strong one, the one helping you. I don't like you seeing me like this, weak and pathetic."

"Those are two words I would never use to describe you, and I never want to hear you say them again about yourself. Are we clear?"

Stephanie didn't answer. She just nodded her acquiescence.

"Good. Now I don't know about you, but I'm exhausted. Let's go to sleep and get some rest."

"I was in such a rush to get here I didn't pack a bag. I don't have anything with me."

"That's okay, I'll find something for you." Meredith's hand slipped into her own and drew her across the room toward the bedroom. "You allowed me to sleep with you when I was scared so now, I'm returning the favour. Besides, I sleep better when you're next to me."

†

The ringing of her phone woke Stephanie from her deep sleep. She opened her eyes, and when she realised she was snuggled within Meredith's arms, she let out a contented sigh.

"Are you going to get that?" Meredith asked, her voice groggy with sleep. "Morning, by the way."

"Good morning."

She reluctantly slid out of Meredith's arms, and as she swung her legs over the side of the bed to sit up she grabbed her mobile from the nightstand.

"It's Joe." Taking a deep breath, she accepted the call. "Hello."

"I know we had a fight, but I didn't think you were the type of person to blow off work. Where are you?"

Any thoughts of apologising to Joe went straight out of Stephanie's mind. To even think that she would be in today after what happened two days ago was crazy. To start with, her hand was still in agony and she still couldn't forget the words he had said.

"I'm in Bristol."

"Bristol?"

She didn't reply, waiting for Joe to connect the dots. It didn't take him long.

"You're with her? What the hell are you thinking?"

"I'm only going to say this once. Where I go and what I do and who I do it with is none of your business and I don't want to discuss it."

She could feel Meredith shift on the bed, the warmth she felt inside when she settled behind her, legs either side of hers, and arms encircling her waist, made her feel like she was home. Somehow over the last few months, Meredith had become her anchor, her touchstone, and nobody was going to take that away from her, not even Joe.

"Steph, we've been friends for years. I think I know you pretty well, and this isn't right."

"I'm sorry you feel that way, but I have to do what I need to do."

"Fine. Until you come to your senses you are not welcome in my home. Call me when that happens."

The line disconnected, and she threw her phone back onto the nightstand. She bowed her head, a deep sadness sweeping through her. She wished it hadn't come to this, but she was no more responsible for Joe's actions than he was hers.

"What did he say?"

She didn't answer for a few moments, collecting her thoughts. Finally, she looked up and tilted her head to the side to look at Meredith.

"I don't suppose you know any good estate agents?"

Meredith looked at her confused. "Well, obviously I think I'm pretty good, but I don't know any in York."

Stephanie let out a chuckle. "It's a good job I was talking about Bristol, then."

Meredith shifted out from behind her and stood. Stephanie couldn't help but admire how sexy she looked, standing there with her hands on her hips, wearing nothing but tight boxers and a pale-blue tank top. The bruises had healed months ago, but the scars were still visible on her body. They did not detract from the glorious vision in front of her. As if sensing Stephanie's awareness of her, Meredith quickly moved to grab her nightgown from the back of the door.

Stephanie realised her mistake, Meredith probably thought she was staring at her in horror. Stephanie knew of all the injuries she had sustained from West, and the last time she had seen Meredith naked she had been covered with bruises and blood. Meredith didn't know Stephanie thought her a wonder, a beauty to behold, not a victim.

Before Meredith could reach the door, Stephanie stood and got in her way. She held her by the shoulders, stopping her from passing, dipping her head to capture Meredith's gaze with her own.

"Please don't. You have nothing to hide from me. You're beautiful."

"No, I'm not. I'm hideous."

"I have scars too. They don't make you who you are." She ran her hands down Meredith's arms until she held her hands, ignoring the pain in her own hand. "Don't you dare say that again! You're beautiful inside and out, and anybody who doesn't see that isn't worth your time."

Meredith sagged against her, and nodding her head, she whispered, "Thank you. You make me believe that I am beautiful."

"It's because it's true."

Meredith took a step back from her and asked, "Why do you need an estate agent here?"

"Joe basically said to stay away from him until I come to my senses. He's not happy I'm here so I'm guessing I need to find a new job. And considering I live at the same place as the gallery, I will need to find somewhere else to live."

"So why here?"

Stephanie shook her head at Meredith's question. Wasn't it obvious?

"Because you're here."

"You can't upend your whole life and move down here just because I live here."

"I have no life up there. Apart from Joe and Fiona, I have no real friends. And now my job has gone and so has my home. I can think of no better reason to move here than you." She walked up to Meredith and took her hands again. "I want to get to know you better. Trying to have any kind of relationship over technology isn't enough. I want to be able to see you, have meals with you, talk over coffee. I can't do any of that if I'm hundreds of miles away."

"But what if it doesn't work out? What if we're both not ready for this?"

"We'll just have to make sure that it does work. Even if we can only be friends, I'd be happy. I need you in my life in whatever capacity you're comfortable with."

She could see Meredith thinking over what she had said, and when a giant smile lit up her face, Stephanie knew she had her answer.

"We better get dressed and head to the office. We have some house hunting to do." Meredith turned away but quickly looked back. "Can you afford this?"

"I have some savings, it's fine."

"Places aren't cheap down here."

What Meredith didn't know was that Stephanie had received a trust fund from her mother's estate when she turned twenty-one. She hadn't spent a penny of it over the years as she felt wrong about spending money that came because her mother had died. She thought now was as good a time as any to make an investment in her future. Hopefully a future with Meredith.

"Get dressed," Stephanie said, a grin on her face.

CHAPTER SEVENTEEN

Meredith and Stephanie stood together in Meredith's kitchen, chopping vegetables they had bought from the local shop for their dinner. They had had a hectic day driving around some of the housing properties that Meredith had on her books. She wasn't lying when she said her clients were all high-end. Many times, Meredith caught the look of awe from Stephanie as she wandered around some of the homes. She was beginning to think they would never find something Stephanie would be comfortable purchasing when they pulled up to a three-bedroom cottage in the countryside that sat on two acres of land. Stephanie had fallen in love with it straight away. It sat high up on a hill and overlooked nothing but farmland and trees. She had commented on how it matched her need for privacy and how the views were breath-taking.

"Are you sure you can afford the cottage?" Meredith asked as she placed carrots in the steamer. Stephanie had yet to mention her budget for buying the property and Meredith was concerned it was higher than she could afford.

"I told you, I have some savings."

Meredith put on her best stern look, hoping to get an honest answer. It must have worked as she watched Stephanie let out a deep breath and turn to face her, resting her backside against the countertop.

"When my mum died, her life insurance was put into a trust fund for me to have when I turned twenty-one. I haven't spent any." Stephanie briefly closed her eyes and shook her head. "I don't know why, but I never felt right about spending it. I think my mum would be pleased I'm investing it in the property." She glanced up into Meredith's eyes. "And my future."

Meredith couldn't miss the look of pure adoration directed her way. Things between them were moving quickly, and she had to constantly fight the need to wrap herself up in Stephanie's arms. She needed to be sure this was the right thing for them both. Considering Stephanie was upending her whole life to be near Meredith, it was a lot of pressure on her to make this work.

"It's okay," Stephanie said. "As I said, I'm happy just being your friend. You don't need to worry about any of this."

"Since when did you become a mind reader?"

"It's one of many superpowers."

Meredith got lost in her eyes and couldn't fight the magnetic pull. She closed the distance between them, intent on kissing those gorgeous lips. She could see Stephanie's cheeks flush. She obviously knew Meredith's intentions. Less than six inches separated them and just as Meredith went on her tiptoes to close the gap, her mobile rang.

"Shit." She pulled away quickly and ran into the living room to grab her phone off the couch. "Hi, Dad," she said, once she connected the call.

"Hello, sweetie. Your mum wanted me to check up on you. Make sure you're okay. We've not heard from you for a while and you know how we worry."

Meredith berated herself. She hadn't realised how her daily calls turning into no communication in two weeks would upset them. Of course, it would. The last time they hadn't heard from her, she had been kidnapped.

"I'm so sorry, Dad. Things have been a little crazy the last few weeks."

"It's okay. We know you have your own life down there, we just need to make sure you're okay."

Meredith took a seat in her comfortable armchair and watched Stephanie in the kitchen, still chopping vegetables. She was chopping with more force than necessary, her frustration at being interrupted clearly visible.

Meredith debated whether to tell her dad about Stephanie and decided she had nothing to hide. Surely, he would understand. He was her dad after all.

"I do need to tell you guys something."

"Hang on. Let me put you on speaker and get your mother."

The phone rustled with the sounds of her father moving around, and then she heard her mother.

"Hi, Mum."

"It's good to hear your voice. How are you?"

"I'm fine. Listen, I was just telling Dad, I need to speak with you about something."

"What is it, dear?" her father asked.

She took a deep breath, and whilst focusing on Stephanie's back, she said, "I've met someone. She's become really special to me and I think I may be falling in love with her."

Stephanie's head whipped around, a slow smile blossoming on her face. She put the knife down and walked over to where Meredith was sitting. She held out her hand and Meredith took it as Stephanie knelt in front of her.

"What about Kathleen?" her father asked.

She watched as Stephanie's gaze hardened. She moved the phone from her ear and whispered, "It's okay." Stephanie visibly relaxed. Meredith was humbled to know she had the strength to calm Stephanie just as Stephanie calmed her when she needed it.

She put the phone back to her ear. "I've spoken to Kath and we both agreed it's over. She's having a hard time with this and we're not the same people we were before I was taken. We're both okay with it."

"Well, who is this new person?"

This was going to be the hard part. Taking all the strength she could find from Stephanie, she said, "Do you remember I told you about a woman who was in the same room as me when I was taken?"

"Yes," her parents replied at the same time.

"Well, her name is Stephanie and we have become really close in the last three months. We've talked quite a lot and gotten to know each other and find we both want to see where this can go."

The line remained silent and she started to panic. Perhaps this was a bad idea. Perhaps they'd react the same way Joe had. Her mother was the first to recover.

"Are you sure about this?"

"Yes."

"Then I guess we can't wait to meet her."

Meredith dropped the phone as tears burst forth from her eyes. Stephanie handed it back to her whilst pulling her into a hug.

"Thank you, Mum, for saying that," she said over Stephanie's shoulder.

"For Heaven's sake, dear. What did you expect us to say?"

"I don't know. I guess I was worried you might think I'm crazy."

"We've always thought that, but we love you anyway," her father quipped. "Sweetheart, people find love in all sorts of places. Who are we to question how and when that happens, as long as it happens, and you're happy. That's all we want."

Stephanie pulled back and wiped the tears away from Meredith's cheeks with her sleeves.

"Thanks, Dad. You have no idea how much that means to me."

"We love you."

"I love you, too."

"Well, we'll leave you to your evening. We have reservations at a new steakhouse in Manhattan. Apparently, the chef is Michelin starred."

"Okay. I'll call you on the weekend."

Meredith disconnected the call and slumped back into the chair. She glanced shyly at Stephanie, who had an unreadable look on her face.

"You okay?"

Stephanie nodded.

"I guess you heard all that."

She nodded again.

"What is it?" Meredith asked.

"Did you mean it?"

"The falling in love part?"

A nod.

"Yes."

Stephanie nodded one more time, stood up, and strode into the kitchen. She began prepping the rest of their dinner.

Meredith was at a loss. She had thought Stephanie would be overjoyed at her declaration. Well, yeah, she didn't exactly declare her undying love, but it was a start, wasn't it? Wasn't this everything Stephanie had hoped for? Hadn't she said she wanted to see where things could go with them?

Deciding the only way to answer her own questions was to confront Stephanie, Meredith stood and walked into the kitchen. Stephanie's back was toward her, her movements jerky and tense.

"What's going on? Steph?"

"Nothing. I'm fine."

"Well, you don't look fine." Meredith reached her hand out and gently laid it on her shoulder. "Talk to me."

Stephanie slowly turned around with a smile on her face, but with tears on her cheeks.

"I had no idea how hearing those words could make me so damn happy. I always thought no one would ever love me like that, and now it's not just some strange emotion I can't understand. It's real, and I just feel so...lucky."

Meredith closed the distance between them and hugged her tightly. "It's real and all true. I'm falling in love with you."

Stephanie pulled back and ever so slowly lowered her mouth to hers. All of Meredith's thoughts left her in that one instant. She opened her mouth fully and allowed Stephanie's tongue to tenderly touch her own. Never had she felt such a swell of passion and desire. She grabbed hold of Stephanie's shirt and pulled her in tighter, their kiss growing hungrier by the second.

After a few minutes of exploring and acquainting their mouths with each other, Meredith pulled back.

"That was..."

"Amazing," Stephanie finished. "Jesus, Mare. I thought my head was going to explode."

Meredith shook her head and slumped against Stephanie's strong chest. Yes, it was amazing, and it confirmed for her that the attraction she was feeling was real. It didn't matter how they met, they had, and it was up to them what happened from now.

"I guess we need to finish dinner," Meredith said.

"Yes, in a minute. I want to kiss you again."

"Sounds like a plan."

†

Dinner had finished an hour ago and now they were sitting opposite each other on the floor, either side of the coffee table, playing poker. It had been a pleasant meal between them, sharing gentle touching of hands and shy looks. Stephanie hadn't said much whilst eating and Meredith could tell she was lost in thought. This was a new development for both of them, one Meredith wasn't expecting to happen, at least not for a while. The more time they spent together, the more Meredith knew how much she had grown fond of Stephanie. She was done procrastinating about the situation of how they met, and she decided to listen to her dad's words. It didn't matter how they met, only that they had.

Meredith looked up at Stephanie and gently squeezed her thigh under the table where her hand rested just above her knee. "You okay?"

"Yeah, I'm good." Stephanie checked on her turn to bet and so did Meredith. Once the cards were face-up Stephanie let out a laugh. "You're really bad at this, aren't you?"

Meredith groaned, and said, "I swear to God you're cheating."

"Nah, I've just played a lot of games in my time."

Meredith took note of the faraway look in Stephanie's eyes and asked again, "Are you sure you're okay?"

"Joe was the one who taught me how to play poker. He'd have poker night around his house at least twice a month and it wasn't long before I was beating him and Fiona." She picked up the cards and shuffled them. As she dealt them out again, she said, "I guess the way I was, at hiding my emotions, made it easy for me to bluff my hands."

"You miss him, don't you?"

"I'm sorry if I've been quiet tonight, but how your mum and dad accepted what you told them made me feel kind of sad about Joe." Stephanie placed her blind before checking her cards, and after Meredith placed the big blind, she glanced at the two cards in front of her. "I don't understand

161

how he could be so against this." She placed a modest bet. "He keeps on at me to express my feelings and not to bottle things up. I thought he would be happy that I'm finally feeling things, good things."

Meredith upped the ante, hoping she could bluff with her seven of hearts and two of diamonds. She never was a very good poker player and she prayed she could get by on bluffing alone. "He'll come around, he loves you." The next card was dealt, and she couldn't help but groan as a queen was laid down. "Why don't you give him a call?"

"I tried earlier when you were in the shower before dinner. He didn't answer. I thought maybe Fiona would have at least texted me to see how I am, but she hasn't."

"I know she is your friend too, but Joe's her husband. She probably doesn't want to get stuck in the middle, and at the end of the day, spouses come first."

Stephanie shot her an angry look and she threw her cards down, clearly not happy with Meredith. "Even when he's in the fucking wrong? He was the one who was out of line. I defended you and you're taking his side?"

Meredith could see why she would think that. After all, Stephanie didn't have many people on her side, and she had no experience in relationships. However, she was wrong, Meredith wasn't on his side, she was trying to see it from all perspectives.

"Steph, this isn't about taking his side. I'm just telling you how Fiona probably feels. As you say, you defended me and took my side in all this, she's probably doing the same."

Stephanie scrubbed her hands over her face and looked up at Meredith sheepishly. "I'm sorry. It's just all bullshit. Why can't he just let me be happy?"

"I'm going to pack this all away as you're clearly not in the mood anymore, and it will save me losing any more chips." She picked up the cards and placed them back in their box. "You're going to be paying the asking price for the cottage and are paying cash, so hopefully the contracts won't take long to exchange, but it will still be a few weeks. What will you do in the meantime?"

Stephanie stood from the floor and went into the kitchen and grabbed two beers they had bought to go with dinner. Coming back into the room, she gave one to Meredith.

"Well, I can't keep wearing your stuff, so I will need to go back up there to grab some things. I guess I'll take a drive up there tomorrow and pack away my belongings and stick them in a storage unit." She sat on the couch and put her bare feet up on the coffee table.

Meredith returned the poker chips and cards back to the sideboard below the lounge window and joined Stephanie on the sofa. She took the proffered beer from Stephanie's outstretched hand and took a long swallow. She was going to suggest something that was totally crazy, but to her it made sense. From the moment they met they had formed a close bond, and to her, it seemed silly for Stephanie to fork out thousands of pounds if she didn't need to.

"This apartment is pretty big. I've got three bedrooms and I'm sure there's plenty enough room for both of us."

"Are you suggesting I move in with you?"

Meredith took a deep breath and let it out slowly. "I'm not saying we live together in a partner kind of way, more like roommates. You can have two of the rooms for yourself and we won't need to spend all our time together if you don't want to."

Stephanie shifted in her seat to face Meredith properly and took hold of her free hand. "We're putting the offer in on the cottage tomorrow, and until it completes, I can stay in a B&B."

"I know what you're saying, however, it just seems silly to me for you to buy something when you could just stay here. And you know, if at any point it doesn't work out between us, you'll be free to go wherever you want."

"Two hours ago, you were saying you were falling in love with me and now you're saying we might not work out? I'm confused."

Meredith kissed the back of Stephanie's hand, a soft smile on her face. "I'm not saying we are not going to work out. I'm just saying if something does go wrong, you wouldn't be tied to Bristol. And besides, I'd prefer it if you were here."

Stephanie didn't answer for a while. She slowly sipped her beer and stared off into space. The silence was killing Meredith. It probably was totally crazy to ask her to move in, but if one thing being in that place taught her, it was that life was short and to take advantage of every opportunity. She knew without a doubt Stephanie was a special woman, a woman she had fallen in love with.

Eventually, the silence was broken when Stephanie whispered a simple but quiet, "Yes."

"Yes?"

Stephanie leaned forward and pressed her lips to Meredith's.

"I would love to move into your spare room." She pulled back and held her gaze. "But I will be paying rent and half of the bills. And don't argue with me on this. It's either that or a bed and breakfast."

Meredith smiled and kissed her again. "You drive a hard bargain. I do have one request, though."

"Oh, you do, do you? And what would that be, my lady?"

"You teach me how to play poker, so I can win."

"Deal."

CHAPTER EIGHTEEN

The next morning found them in Stephanie's rented BMW, heading toward York. They had both slept soundly the night before, and as had become their habit over the last few nights, they shared Meredith's bed. They had kissed a few times, and Stephanie was okay with that. She didn't feel the need for more intimate contact between them. What she had told Joe and Meredith in the past about being over her ordeal with Jameson West was true, and even though she might be ready to take their relationship to the next level, she was sure Meredith wasn't.

She took her attention off the road for a second and glanced at Meredith, who was sitting in the passenger seat next to her. "Are you sure you are all right coming back to York with me?"

"Yes, why do you ask?"

"No reason, except you look a little pale."

"To be honest, I am feeling a little panicky. This is the same route I took back in October."

"Shit, Meredith. If you want, I can go a different way." Stephanie felt like an idiot. She should have known this would be hard for Meredith. After all, this was the first time she had been back here since the kidnapping, and God only knew what kind of memories this was bringing back for her.

"No, it's fine. I need to work through this."

They settled into a companionable silence for the next twenty miles until Stephanie pulled off the main road and headed down a country lane. She could clearly hear Meredith's breathing increase, and out of the corner of her eye, Stephanie saw her rapidly tapping her hand on her thigh.

"Stop!" Meredith shouted.

"What is it? What's the matter?" Stephanie slammed on the brakes and coasted to the side of the road.

"This is the spot. This is where I was taken." Meredith stared out of the windshield, eyes wide, her face ashen. She got out of the car and slammed the door behind her. She walked to the front of the car and sank to her knees, holding her head in her hands.

Stephanie hesitated for only a second and then she was out of the car, rushing to Meredith's side. She gathered Meredith in her arms and held her while she wept.

"I knew this was a bad idea, I'm so sorry."

Through her tears Meredith whispered, "It's not your fault. I knew this would happen. I could feel my anxiety getting worse the closer we got to York, but it wasn't until you pulled off onto this road that my panic hit me full force."

"I should have come here by myself, please forgive me."

Meredith looked up into her eyes and smiled. "There is nothing to forgive. He is the one who made me feel this way, not you." She gathered herself together, wiping the tears from her eyes, and stood, bringing Stephanie with her.

"Let's get back in the car. My jeans are filthy."

They settled back into their seats, but Stephanie didn't pull away. She took Meredith's hand. "It will get better, I promise."

"I just now realised you've never told me how he managed to kidnap you. In all our time there, and since then, you have never mentioned it. How come?"

Stephanie turned away from her and stared out of the windshield, thinking back to her own kidnapping. She surmised the reason she never told anyone was because she wasn't proud of her actions that night.

"I guess I blame myself for that. I put myself in a dangerous situation and my behaviour caused it to happen."

"What are you talking about? He's a psycho, how could any of it be your fault?"

Stephanie looked back into Meredith's eyes and the love and encouragement she saw in her face made her realise Meredith would never think badly of her. Meredith had been nothing but supportive since they met. Stephanie knew she could trust her.

"I went to a club with Joe that night and I got completely wasted. I'm not talking about your regular drunkenness, but completely out of it. I only live about a fifteen-minute walk from the club, which is around the corner from the high street, so I decided to walk home. Joe wanted me to get into a taxi, but I blew him off and told him I would be fine. I had made it back to the gallery, and as I turned down the alley behind to get to the apartment, West hit me across the face with something, and the next thing I remember is waking up next to you."

"That doesn't mean it was your fault. I mean, yeah, it probably wasn't wise to walk home in that state, but he had no right to attack you and kidnap you."

Stephanie started the car and pulled away from the edge of the road, intent on carrying on their journey. If she concentrated on driving, she might be able to forget the shame and embarrassment she felt over allowing him to surprise her. She felt Meredith's hand squeeze her shoulder as she tried hard not to cry. She couldn't decide which was better, not feeling anything at all, and being envious of people who could, or being able to experience emotions, but have no control over which ones came out and when. It was a learning curve, and one she didn't think she would be able to master for a long time.

"I guess I blame myself for getting hurt the same way I blame myself for my mother's death."

"What do you mean? I thought that was a freak accident?"

Stephanie thought back to an argument with her father a few months before he dropped her off at the foster home. She had accidentally broken one of his expensive fishing rods and he flew into a rage at her, saying she was useless, always ruining everything, and eventually telling her she was the one who caused the accident that killed her mum.

"Apparently I was in the backseat messing around and I managed to unclip the seatbelt that was holding me in my car seat. My mum turned around to try to get me to put it back on and she lost control of the car. My dad told me if I hadn't been pissing about, she would still be alive, and he wouldn't be stuck with a brat like me." The tears did fall now, she didn't care. She angrily wiped them away, keeping her eyes focused on the road ahead. She didn't want to cause another accident and kill somebody else that she loved.

"Sweetheart. That wasn't your fault. You were practically a baby. Your mum could have pulled over to the side of the road and clipped you back in safely, but she didn't. You can't blame yourself for that any more than you can blame yourself for Jameson West taking you."

"No, you're wrong. It was my actions that led to both events happening and nothing you say is going to change that."

Stephanie turned down another country road and eventually the fields became more populated with houses and bungalows. They were only a few miles now from the city centre and the sooner they got there the better. Stephanie liked to put things in boxes in her mind and leave them there, unopened. All this talk about her mother and West brought thoughts to the surface she didn't want to deal with. The sooner she could stuff them back into their respective boxes the better.

"I see you have your mind set on feeling that way," Meredith said. "But in time, I am going to make sure you understand that neither event was your fault. But thank you for telling me, I think I understand you a bit better now."

Stephanie didn't reply. She gripped the wheel tighter and continued to drive.

†

Stephanie opened the door to the gallery, and the little bell above the door tinkled, announcing their presence to Joe who was standing behind the counter. Stephanie was

170

nervous. This was the first time she had spoken to him in a week. He glanced up and smiled before realising who was at the door, and his friendly demeanour shifted into indifference. She reached behind and grabbed hold of Meredith's hand, pulling her along as they approached Joe.

"Joe, I'd like you to meet Meredith. Meredith, this is Joe."

Meredith put her hand out. "It's nice to meet you, I have heard a lot about you."

Stephanie watched as Joe eyed Meredith suspiciously for a few moments before eventually putting his hand into hers, giving it a quick shake.

"I've heard a lot about you, too." He turned to Stephanie. "How have you been?"

"Not too bad." She turned to Meredith and gave her a pleading look. She knew this was going to be hard and she hoped Meredith would help her out.

She didn't.

"I'm going to go and look at some of the art work," Meredith said. "Let me know when you're ready to go up." She gave Stephanie a reassuring smile and went back to the front of the gallery to give them some privacy.

Stephanie turned back to Joe, trying to gauge his reaction to Meredith being here. She wanted to apologise for hitting him the other day, but somehow, she just couldn't find the words. She was saved from her reverie by Joe who spoke first.

"Listen, Squirt. I've been talking to Fiona and she has made me realise that I was out of line. I shouldn't have said what I did and I'm sorry."

"I'm sorry too. I shouldn't have hit you, but I couldn't let you talk about her that way." She looked over her shoulder at

171

Meredith who was studying intently a selection of pencil drawings. She smiled to herself.

"Does she know they are yours?" Joe asked.

"No, I haven't really told her about my artwork. She knows I have a degree in art, but I don't think she realises I do my own stuff."

"Well, she seems to like them. Rather strange that out of all the pieces that are here, it's yours that have captured her attention. Wait here a minute, I need to go make a sale." He came around the side of the counter and was striding toward Meredith before Stephanie even had a chance to think.

Stephanie was frozen to the spot. God only knew what he was going to say to her, she just hoped he behaved. Her panic settled when Meredith glanced over at her and smiled, then let out a small chuckle. Joe laughed, too, as he began to remove the three seven-by-five frames from the wall. They came back over to the counter and Joe set about wrapping the frames in bubble wrap and packaging paper.

"You never told me you were such a good artist."

"You don't have to pay for them," Stephanie said. "You can have them as a gift."

Meredith smiled. "Don't worry, I've been given a discount."

Joe laughed again and handed Meredith her purchase. Stephanie looked between the two and knew something suspicious was going on. Before she had a chance to question them both Joe asked, "So what brings you here, I take it you're not coming back to work?" He took Meredith's credit card and completed the transaction.

Stephanie took a deep breath and steadied herself. This was going to be difficult to say so she took hold of

Meredith's hand and decided the best way to break the news to him was to blurt it out.

"I have decided, well, we have decided, that I am going to move to Bristol and we are going to see what we have between us." She kept eye contact with him while he processed her statement. Sometimes he was hard to read, and this was one of those times. He took a few minutes looking from her to Meredith and back again and she felt her palms sweat. She let go of Meredith's hand and wiped them both on her jeans. "Say something, this is killing me."

"I still have the bruises from the last time I said something, so for now, I think I'll keep quiet." He gave a small chuckle and Stephanie was relieved he wasn't so angry that he couldn't make a joke.

"I'm sorry I'm going to be leaving you without a manager, but this is something I need to do."

Joe focused his attention on Meredith. "Is this what you want also?"

Meredith looked at her, and Stephanie could see nothing but love and acceptance in her face. "Yes." She looked back at Joe and continued. "Stephanie is a really special person and she has become important to me in more ways than I could have imagined. I can't fathom not having her in my life."

Joe seemed satisfied with the answer and a smile broke out on his face. The door to the gallery jingled as a prospective customer walked in. "I need to get back to work."

"Sorry. One of the reasons why we are here is so I can pack my things."

"Are you planning to head back to Bristol tonight? Because it would be great if you could come and have dinner with Fiona and myself. You can stay the night and get a head start early in the morning. Of course, you're invited too, Meredith."

"That okay with you, Meredith?"

"If we are back home by three, then yes, as I have a counselling appointment. I would be delighted to spend the evening with you and your wife."

"Cool. Come to see us around seven o'clock."

The customer signalled Joe's attention. He rushed off to aid the customer and Stephanie took Meredith's hand again and led her through the back room and up into her apartment.

"It shouldn't take me too long to pack. I don't have much. Most of the furniture is Joe's and anything we can't fit in the car I can have shipped."

"Are you sure about this?" Meredith fidgeted from foot to foot, her nerves palpable. "What I said to Joe downstairs is true; however, if you have even the slightest doubt, please let me know now."

"I have never been surer about anything in my life." Stephanie slowly went to her and kissed her on the lips. Meredith's skin flushed. The corners of her mouth turned up into a soft smile.

"Thank you."

"Let's start packing."

She moved away from Meredith, going into the small kitchen to start unloading her pots and pans from the cupboards. Curiosity got the better of her.

"So, um, what did Joe say to you when he came over to you." She hoped it came out as casual, however, the stumbling over her words didn't go unnoticed by her or Meredith.

"Oh, nothing much." Meredith came into the kitchen also, a slight smirk on her face. "Don't worry, he behaved himself." She must have realised how worried Stephanie was because she followed up. "He apologised for the things he said about me and then we were talking about your drawings. You have quite a unique style."

Stephanie blew out a breath and faced her. "I haven't really done much in the last few years, what with working with Joe, but back when I did my degree, I was doodling quite a lot."

"I wouldn't call it doodling. There is something very dark and beautiful about the way you capture your subject. Do you have any more? I would love to see them."

Stephanie brushed passed Meredith and went into her bedroom, coming back a few moments later with a sketchpad in hand. She gave it to Meredith.

"Some of these are pretty bad, but go ahead, take a look." She left Meredith in the kitchen, browsing her sketchpad while she popped back downstairs to ask Joe if he had any boxes she could use. A few minutes later she came back into the kitchen and stopped dead in her tracks. Meredith was staring at one of her drawings and Stephanie could clearly see the tears in her eyes.

"What's the matter?"

Meredith turned to her and held up a sketch of a young girl sat in the dark, knees drawn to her chest, her face turned to the artist. The pain on the girl's face was clear.

"This is you, isn't it?"

Stephanie put down the boxes and walked over to Meredith, quickly glancing at the sketch and back to her. "Yes. I think I was about twenty-two when I drew that."

Meredith reached out a hand and placed it on her cheek, softly stroking the skin with her thumb. "Oh, sweetheart, you must have been so lonely growing up."

"It's okay. Everything that has happened to me has led me to you." Stephanie smiled.

"But still, I'm so sorry you had no one."

Before Stephanie could get overemotional, she pulled back and scrubbed her hands over her face. "Now isn't the time to be getting into all that, we have packing to do."

CHAPTER NINETEEN

"Thank you, Fiona," Meredith said. "That was delicious." She placed her knife and fork down onto the plate and rubbed her stomach. "I'm stuffed."

"I have to agree," Stephanie said. "Fiona, you have outdone yourself."

The four of them sat around Joe and Fiona's dining room table. It was eight thirty at night and Meredith and Stephanie had arrived an hour earlier. After finishing packing up Stephanie's things, they had driven around York with Stephanie playing tour guide. They had a lovely afternoon walking around the area in the late August sun.

"Well, I didn't get much notice you were coming so I couldn't do anything too fancy, but nothing beats chilli." Fiona stood, picking up her plate.

"Sit." Meredith motioned to the table. "I'll get this as you cooked."

"I'll help," Joe said as he collected the plate Fiona was still holding. He looked from Stephanie to his wife. "Maybe you two can catch up without us earwigging." He winked at Fiona and gave her a loving smile that in turn made Meredith smile too. It was clear how much they loved each other, and she couldn't help but glance at Stephanie who was watching her. She felt her cheeks heat in response to the sexy smile directed her way.

She cleared her throat and, after stacking up some of the tableware, she followed Joe into the kitchen. He opened the dishwasher and began placing the plates into the rack. She stood next to him, passing him the things she held. After a few moments of silence, she asked, "So, do I pass the test?"

His actions stilled as he glanced at her. "Don't know what you mean." He continued filling the dishwasher.

"Joe..." She put her hand on his arm, pleased with herself that her fear of touch was gradually disappearing, and waited until he straightened and faced her. She dropped her hand and said, "I know you have concerns over Steph and me, and I fully understand them. We have reservations too, but it would mean a lot if we had your blessing. This is new to her and having your support would mean the world."

Joe studied her face for a moment, looking for what she didn't know. He surprised her when he gently traced the thin, fading scar on her cheek. She kept still, not letting her anxiety get the better of her. He withdrew his hand and ran his fingers through his hair, clearly frustrated.

"I like you, Meredith, I really do. I can see why Steph has fallen for you. After the things you've both been through, I can see she was right. You are a strong person and it upsets me you went through it, and her."

A small smile formed on her lips as Meredith thought he had finally accepted their relationship. He may have given his blessings earlier in the gallery, but she needed to make sure. It looked like he had been sincere earlier, however, he had more to say.

"But I can't say I'm thrilled about her moving to Bristol with you. Before you say anything, let me finish. She had an awful start to life and was only just beginning to get her head sorted. She has friends and a decent job. She's like my sister and I'd do anything to protect her. I wasn't there for her when that prick took her, and I let her down. I won't let that happen again. I won't have her getting hurt again by anyone and if that means I have to upset her to protect her, then I will."

Meredith let his words sink in, trying to figure out how to convince him she wasn't going to hurt Stephanie. She knew she couldn't say anything to change his mind. Instead, she was honest with him.

"I can't promise things will always be easy between us, and she might get hurt sometimes, but what I can do is promise that I will do whatever it takes to protect her and not hurt her intentionally. I love her, and if I do something to hurt her, I'll be the first person knocking on your door, so you can kick my ass."

He stared at her for a moment, then let out a chuckle. "Good enough." He smiled and shook his head, turning serious again. "Please take care of her."

"I will."

Stephanie came into the kitchen. "Hey, what's taking so long? I want my dessert."

"Sorry, Squirt. I was just asking her about her intentions toward you."

Stephanie looked from one to the other. "You better not have upset her, Joe."

Meredith went to Stephanie's side and placed an arm around her waist. She kissed her cheek. "Don't worry. He was just being a big brother."

Stephanie didn't look convinced and Meredith knew she would be asked about it later. For now, though, she headed back into the dining room to finish clearing the table, determined to enjoy the rest of the evening. Joe's worries and doubts were not far from her mind.

†

Later that night Stephanie and Meredith were lying in bed together in Joe's spare bedroom. Meredith's head rested on Stephanie's shoulder, her arm draped over her waist. It was close to midnight and Meredith was shattered. It had been a very long day and she was looking forward to a good night's rest and she knew sleeping in Stephanie's arms would help her relax. Hopefully, tonight would be nightmare free. She felt Stephanie tighten her hold on her and she knew without asking what was on her mind. After they had gone back into the dining room Stephanie had been quiet, and although she still joined in on the conversations and joking around, Meredith could tell the scene in the kitchen was playing heavily on her mind.

"Do you want to talk about it or are you just going to continue to sulk?"

"I'm not sulking."

180

Meredith kissed her shoulder and waited until Stephanie was ready to talk. She didn't have to wait long.

"I guess I'm still annoyed at Joe for warning you off again."

Meredith sat up and entwined her fingers with Stephanie's. "He didn't warn me off." At Stephanie's raised eyebrows, she said, "He didn't, I promise. He just wanted to make sure that I wasn't going to hurt you. He loves you. I'd be worried if he didn't say anything."

Stephanie shuffled up the bed into a sitting position and blew out a breath. "I guess I can understand his fears. I sometimes wonder if you'll hurt me too." Meredith pulled back and Stephanie must have realised how that sounded as she quickly reached for her to stop her leaving the bed. "That's not what I meant, Meredith. Please just let me explain."

Meredith gazed at her and the panic on her face didn't go unnoticed. She had her reservations about their relationship too, but she knew in her heart she loved Stephanie and would do whatever it took to make it work between them. To hear that Stephanie thought she might hurt her tore her up. She thought they were in the same place, that although they met under difficult circumstances, their attraction to each other was real. Meredith knew Stephanie would never hurt her, why didn't Stephanie feel the same? She pushed aside her fear of what Stephanie was about to say.

"Okay, talk to me." Meredith settled next to her against the headboard and held her hand.

"I know we have something special, but I also know the things you're struggling with and how we met. I just have this fear that one day you'll wake up and you won't need me anymore."

"What? What do you think is going on here?" Meredith let go of Stephanie's hand and this time she did get out of bed. She crossed to the other side of the small room and sat back on an ornate dressing table. "I told you I was falling in love with you. I've asked you to move in with me. What more can I do to prove to you that I'm serious about us? Do you think I'm just waiting until I'm emotionally and physically healed and I'll then dump you?"

Stephanie said nothing. Her head hung low and she sat very still. She didn't look at Meredith and Meredith feared that that was exactly what she thought.

"You need to explain this to me, Steph, because I'm confused." Eventually, Stephanie looked up and the vulnerability Meredith saw broke her heart. "What is it?" she asked softly.

"Everyone leaves."

Those two words whispered so quietly she strained to hear them, had Meredith striding across the room and gathering Stephanie up into a fierce hug. "Oh, sweetheart. Do you really think that?"

"My heart says no but my dumb head keeps getting in the way. I'm sorry."

Meredith pulled back slightly and captured Stephanie's guarded gaze with her own. "You don't ever need to apologise for feeling something you feel. I don't know what the future holds for us, but I want to go on this journey with you. I have no intention of ever letting you go. I love you." This was the first time she said the words directly, not alluding to it or suggesting she was falling in love. Meredith did love her and Stephanie needed to hear it so she could start believing it. Meredith hugged her again.

"I know I still have some things to work through and so do you, but we're going to do it together, okay?"

Stephanie didn't answer, but Meredith felt her nod against her neck. They sat that way for a while, neither speaking, but holding each other close.

"I love you, too, Mare. So much."

Meredith smiled and allowed the feeling those words had on her to flow through her and settle into her heart.

CHAPTER TWENTY

•

The following morning, Meredith and Stephanie stood next to Stephanie's car, saying goodbye to Joe and Fiona. They all had a simple breakfast of toast and coffee and Meredith was eager to get on the road. She was not looking forward to the six-hour drive back to Bristol. She had her appointment with her counsellor at three that afternoon and she wanted to make sure she was back in plenty of time. Waking up at 6 o'clock that morning had been hard, especially lying in Stephanie's arms. Not soon after their conversation last night they had both fallen into a deep sleep. Meredith hoped the matter was now settled, and Stephanie believed she would never leave her.

Meredith certainly had plenty to talk to her counsellor about. She was looking forward to discussing the recent developments in her relationship with Stephanie, and her feelings toward Jameson West, and the way she was now coping with interacting with people. She had gotten better with coping. She had managed to engage with Joe and had allowed him to touch her cheek, and both times she hadn't flinched. She had been a little panicked, but nowhere near the way she had been before, and she had no fear of an anxiety attack. She was improving and she was pleased.

"Thank you, Fiona, for cooking us dinner and for the bed for a night. I had a wonderful time. You both have to come down to Bristol sometime and we can return the favour."

"It was lovely to meet you. And yes, that would be nice."

Going on her new-found acceptance with people in her personal space, Meredith stepped forward and hugged Fiona. It was easy to do, because Fiona really was a nice person. She could see why Joe fell in love with her. She turned to Stephanie and noticed she was in a quiet conversation with Joe.

Deciding they needed a chance for a proper goodbye, Meredith said, "I'll be in the car." Stephanie nodded and went back to talking with Joe.

She got into the passenger side of the car and waited for Stephanie. Her mobile phone rang and she fished it out of her jeans pocket. She glanced at the caller ID and recognised the number of Detective Walker, the detective who had interviewed her a few months ago after she had arrived home from the hospital. She accepted the call.

"Hello, detective."

"Good morning, Miss Ashcroft. I'm sorry it's so early but I wanted to call you before I got bogged down in work."

"That's okay, I'm up and about anyway."

"Well, I just wanted to let you know a trial date has been set for Jameson West. It's set to begin January fifth, barring any delays. Obviously, you will be called as a witness, as well as the other women he took. The prosecution will be in touch with a time to meet with you to go over what happened and gather any more evidence they may need."

Meredith closed her eyes and tried to settle her heart rate as it thrummed hard in her chest. She refused to have an anxiety attack over this.

"Okay, thank you for calling me and letting me know."

The driver's side door opened and Stephanie stepped inside. She must have seen Meredith's panic as she looked at her questioningly and placed a hand on her thigh.

"I don't particularly want to face him again, but I know this has to be done to put the son of a bitch away."

"I know this will be difficult for you," Detective Walker said. "As it will be for all the witnesses, but we have trained professionals to help you with anything you will need. And don't forget you can call me anytime if you need to."

"Thank you again."

Meredith disconnected the call and placed the phone back in her pocket. She pinched the bridge of her nose and blew out a breath.

"Are you okay?" Stephanie asked.

"I think so." She turned and regarded Stephanie, who was looking at her with a worried look on her face. "Jameson West's trial will begin on the fifth of January. I guess we need to start preparing to face that monster again."

"Well, I for one can't wait to see that sick fucker be sent down." Stephanie started the engine and pulled out of the driveway.

Meredith didn't want to talk about him anymore, she would have to face him soon enough, and she didn't want to spoil the journey home by thinking of him. "So how are you and Joe? Is everything okay between you both now?"

"Yeah, I think we're good. I'm pretty sure Fiona spoke with him again because he didn't rag on me for moving in with you. I also told him I would come back once a month to help him with his accounts as he never really has been any good at the paperwork side of the business. He has a good eye for art, but not for numbers." She chuckled.

"That's good, I'm happy that both of you are working things out." Meredith smiled.

Stephanie steered the car out of Joe's neighbourhood, but she didn't leave the same way they had arrived yesterday. She took the car in a different direction.

"How come you're going this way?" Meredith asked.

"I just thought it best we avoid going down the same road you were taken."

"Thank you. That's very sweet of you."

†

Later that evening Meredith was in the kitchen making a salad for their dinner. She was standing at the stove, frying up some chicken pieces to go on the bed of lettuce and tomatoes that were already on plates on the kitchen counter. Stephanie had spent the last few hours unpacking the few boxes she had brought with her from Joe's and was now in the shower. As Meredith uncorked a bottle of wine, she went over her counselling session in her mind. It had been good, she had enjoyed it. The counsellor was pleased with the progress she was making within herself and the management of her panic attacks, but Meredith knew she still had a long way to go. She accredited her improvement to Stephanie's support. She was positive if Stephanie had not come into her life again, she would probably still be stuck, fearful of touch and unable to go out.

She took the chicken off the heat and spooned it on top of the salads. She poured two glasses of wine, and as she carried the glasses into the lounge, Stephanie came out of the spare bedroom, towel drying her short dark hair.

"Hey, how was the shower?"

"It was amazing. It felt good to get the day's grime off me." Stephanie kissed her on the cheek.

"Well, take a seat, dinner is served." Meredith headed back into the kitchen to grab their salads and cutlery, and as she walked back into the lounge Stephanie was staring at her.

"What?" she asked as she placed the plates on the coffee table.

"Nothing. I was just thinking how beautiful you are."

Meredith felt the heat rise to her cheeks and rolled her eyes when Stephanie chuckled.

"Flattery will get you everywhere." She took a seat and picked up a fork.

"I'm serious. You're gorgeous, Meredith. And thanks for this, it looks great."

Meredith glanced at her, watching as Stephanie dug into her dinner with gusto. "I take it you're hungry?" She laughed as Stephanie tried to talk with her mouth full. "That's a yes then."

"So how did you get on with Doctor Williams? If you don't mind me asking, that is."

"No, that's fine." Meredith took a sip of wine, and after swallowing, she said, "It was good. She thinks I've made tremendous progress but has suggested keeping the regular appointments once a week." She chewed a piece of chicken while she gathered her thoughts. "We spoke a little bit about the upcoming trial and how I feel about that, but mainly we talked about you." She watched as Stephanie's eyebrows rose and the corners of the mouth turned down into a frown. "Don't worry, it was all good."

"Did you discuss my moving in here?"

"Yes, we did. I told her that you had your own room, but to be honest, we would probably end up sleeping in the same bed." She blushed again as Stephanie smirked. "I don't think I'm ready for that yet, Steph." She placed her hands on her lap and looked down at the table, hating that after all the progress she had made, and how much she wanted to be with Stephanie, she still couldn't imagine herself being able to have anyone touch her like that anytime soon. She was surprised when Stephanie tilted her face up with her finger and smiled sweetly at her.

"I'm not ready for that either. Please don't worry, we can wait for as long as it takes for us both to be comfortable with it. But I do like sleeping next to you, it makes me feel safe."

Meredith was dismayed when a lone tear escaped her eye and she angrily swiped it away. Stephanie was always so sweet and always made her feel loved.

"I like having you hold me, too. I don't want to appear selfish, so any time you need space, please just tell me." She didn't want to be clingy even if that was exactly what she was.

"There is nothing selfish about wanting to sleep next to the person you love. And if there was, then I would be selfish too."

Meredith leaned forward to kiss Stephanie, however, before their lips touched, there was a knock at the door. She glanced at the clock, noting it was nearly seven.

"I'll be right back." She pushed back from the table and went to the front door. To say she was shocked when she saw who was on the other side would be an understatement. "What on earth are you doing here?"

Kathleen stood leaning against the doorframe, hands in the pockets of her jeans. She was as beautiful as ever, but this was the most casual Meredith had ever seen her.

"I've missed you," Kathleen said. "I know I wasn't there for you when you needed me, but I have done some thinking and I wanted to apologise to you and see if maybe we could talk."

Meredith didn't know what to say. Kathleen was the last person she expected to see standing at her door asking for forgiveness. Was she hoping they could get back together? If she did then she was crazy. Even if Meredith didn't have feelings for Stephanie, she still wouldn't want to go back to Kathleen.

"Say something, baby." Kathleen reached her hand toward her and Meredith could only watch as she gently pushed a loose strand of her hair behind her ear.

"Meredith? Is everything okay?" Stephanie asked as she walked up behind her. Meredith watched Kathleen's face transform from one of open caring to a scowl, lips pressed into a thin line.

"What is she doing here?" Kathleen seethed.

"I live here," Stephanie said simply as she possessively wrapped an arm around Meredith's waist, ever so slightly pulling her away from Kathleen.

Kathleen glared at Stephanie and then back to Meredith, who still had yet to utter a word.

"I see." She straightened up and ran her hands through her hair, messing the usually perfectly coiffured style. "Well, I just made an idiot out of myself, haven't I?"

Meredith found her voice finally. "I'm sorry. We love each other."

"He really did mess you up, didn't he?" Kathleen snorted, a very unpleasant sound for someone who purported to be a lady. She didn't wait for a response; she turned on her heel and strode away.

Stephanie slowly closed the door and locked it with a soft click. She took Meredith's hand and led her into the lounge and their interrupted meal. Meredith sat in her vacated seat and stared blindly at the coffee table. Stephanie crouched beside her, resting her hands on Meredith's thighs.

"Are you okay?"

Was she? Meredith had no idea. She supposed she would have had to speak to Kathleen at some point, she just hadn't thought the confrontation would be now. She looked up at Stephanie and couldn't help the tears that escaped her eyes.

"Oh, honey. Don't listen to what she said. She has no idea what we went through and how we feel about each other." Stephanie gathered her in her arms and Meredith wept.

"I can't believe she would say that to me. I know we weren't the perfect match, but I thought she loved me, at least at one time. How can she be so cruel?"

Stephanie cupped her cheeks, brushing away her tears. "Please don't listen to her. She isn't worth it."

"I'm suddenly feeling very tired. It's been a long day. Do you mind if I go to bed?"

Meredith didn't give Stephanie a chance to answer as she rose from the sofa and practically ran into her bedroom, closing the door behind her. She collapsed onto her bed and cried.

†

Stephanie stood outside Meredith's bedroom door with her forehead resting on the wood panelling. She could hear her crying softly on the other side. She debated whether to go in or to just leave her be. She decided nothing she could say would help Meredith feel any better. She stepped away from the door and gathered the plates off the coffee table and carried them into the kitchen. As she rinsed them in the sink and stacked them in the dishwasher, her blood boiled. How dare Kathleen come to Meredith's home and talk to her like that! It took all her will power not to hunt her down and whip her ass. Meredith was the kindest, sweetest person she knew, and no one had the right to talk to her like that.

She headed back into the lounge, grabbing the wine bottle off the counter on the way, and slouched into the couch, swigging straight from the bottle. She turned on the television, hoping to drown out the crying she could still hear from Meredith. She wanted to go to her, but who was she kidding? She wasn't emotionally equipped enough to deal with this. Yes, she had made progress in the last three months, since the kidnapping, with dealing and facing her emotions, but she still felt inadequate, especially with someone as fragile as Meredith.

She continued to drink steadily over the next half hour whilst channel surfing, trying to push aside her need to go to Meredith. It had been an incredibly long day and she was exhausted. She polished off the bottle and took it into the kitchen to dispose of. A clearing of the throat startled her from behind and the bottle clanged loudly amongst the other glass in the recycling bin. Stephanie spun around, seeing Meredith standing in the entryway to the kitchen. She looked terrible. Her eyes were red-rimmed and her hair was a mess, strands sticking out in all directions.

"Hey, how are you feeling?" she asked softly, not moving from her side of the kitchen.

"Like I have just been through the emotional wringer."

"I wanted to come in and comfort you, but I didn't know how." Her heart lurched when Meredith's eyes teared up again. She went to her now and gathered her in her arms. "Sweetheart, please don't listen to what she said."

Meredith shook her head against Stephanie's chest. "No, that isn't why I am crying. How could you ever think you wouldn't know how to comfort me? Just being in your arms is all I need." She kissed her gently on the lips. "Please don't question yourself, darling, just do what you feel is right."

"I'm sorry, it's just when you walked out, you were so upset I didn't know what to do."

Meredith took her by the hand and led her toward her bedroom. "All I want is for you to lay down with me and hold me until I forget all about Kathleen's words."

"Now that I can do."

CHAPTER TWENTY-ONE

Meredith was sitting in Carrie's kitchen, nursing a cup of coffee that was rapidly growing cold. Since her breakdown two weeks ago, she had been on edge, but especially the last few days. She thought it was due to Kathleen's words, but on Thursday morning whilst at work, she noticed the date. She realised the anniversary of the kidnapping was coming up in a week, and this had made her agitated. She tried not to take it out on Stephanie, but she couldn't help snapping at her over the stupidest of things, like leaving her shoes by the front door. Stephanie tried her best to placate her, but Meredith could see her own actions were beginning to wear on Stephanie. She supposed she should say what was bugging her, but she didn't want to appear weak, especially after the other weekend. She wanted to speak to her father, however she knew he would be busy with work. She didn't want him worrying about her, so she had rung Carrie and asked to see her.

"You have been here for an hour now," Carrie said. "And as much as I enjoy your company, I can see something is bothering you. What's the matter? Is everything okay with you and Steph?"

Meredith smiled as she thought about Stephanie. Apart from the tension that Meredith had created during the past weeks, things between them were going great. They slept in the same bed every night and they enjoyed their evenings getting to know each other better. Meredith had gone back to work full-time. Although she spent that time in the office, she wasn't quite ready to go out to meet clients, but she was enjoying herself. Stephanie had begun looking for a job and sending her CV off to potential employers. They would laugh and talk, and they were growing closer if that were possible. It was only Meredith's attitude that had marred an otherwise perfect few weeks.

"Me and Steph are great. In fact, I'm surprised at how well her moving in has gone. I have been a little bit prickly toward her recently." Carrie raised her eyebrows and nodded for her to continue. "Do you remember what date I was kidnapped?"

"Of course. That isn't something I'm going to forget any time soon. October fifteenth."

"And what is today's date?"

Carrie scrunched up her face, clearly confused as to why she was asking these questions. Meredith knew the exact moment Carrie realised what she was alluding to. Her mouth formed an O and her eyes went wide. "Eighth of October. It's been a year since you were taken." She reached out her hand and placed it on Meredith's forearm, giving it a slight squeeze. "I'm sorry. No wonder you're out of sorts. What does Stephanie say about all this?"

Meredith looked away, feeling ashamed. She knew what Carrie's reaction would be. "I haven't exactly spoken to her about it yet."

"What? Jesus Christ, Meredith, why on earth would you not speak to her about this? This is obviously a big deal for you, and I imagine it'll be a pretty big deal for her too. Don't forget she went through the same thing."

"I know, I know, you're right. We have always been able to talk about anything, especially what happened in that place, but I just don't know how to explain how I'm feeling." She gazed at Carrie, feeling helpless. She wasn't sure why this was having such an effect on her. It wasn't like West could hurt her anymore, and she knew Stephanie would understand, she just couldn't find the words to explain what was going on. She pushed her cup away and blew out a deep breath.

"Have I told you the trial date has been set yet?" Carrie shook her head. "January fifth. I guess the anniversary of the kidnapping, the news of the trial, and what Kathleen said has made me rattled."

"Kathleen? What does she have to do with any of this?"

"Oh yeah, she came by a couple of weeks ago saying she wanted to get back together." At Carrie's raised eyebrows, she continued, "She wasn't particularly pleased to see Stephanie in the apartment and basically told me that West had fucked my head up."

"Where the hell does she get off speaking to you like that?"

Carrie's anger was palpable, Meredith smiled at her best friend's defense of her. "Yeah, that's what Steph said. I was pretty upset after that little confrontation and had a mini breakdown. Stephanie was amazing and spent the whole night holding me. She doesn't deserve to be treated the way I have been treating her and I know I need to talk to her about the anniversary, but I just don't know how."

Meredith was at a loss. The previous few weeks had been a nightmare because of West. She shook her head: no, he may have made her on edge, and Kathleen hadn't helped, but the weeks were pretty amazing with Stephanie. Meredith needed to apologise to her, she needed to make things right.

"I just can't wait for this whole ordeal to be over with. The sooner he gets sent down, the better."

"Well, I'm here whenever you need me, you know that. But you need to talk to Stephanie. You don't want this to be ruining things between you."

"I know, you're right." Meredith stood from her chair and gathered her belongings. After putting on her coat, she pulled Carrie into a tight hug. "Thank you for listening."

Carrie pulled back and smiled softly at her. "You are very welcome. Let me know when you're both free so we can invite you around for a meal one night."

"Will do."

†

Meredith arrived home a half hour later, and as she walked through the front door, she tripped over Stephanie's trainers, catching herself on the wall before she fell.

"Oh, for Christ's sake!" She kicked the offending items out of her way and went in search of Stephanie. She found her in the lounge, typing away on her laptop. "Is it really that hard for you to understand not to leave your shoes by the door? I nearly broke my neck."

"Good afternoon to you, too." Stephanie put down her laptop on the coffee table and strode over to the front door. She picked up her trainers and threw them through the open doorway of her own bedroom. "Is that better?"

Meredith shook her head, frustrated. Her intention after leaving Carrie's was to come here and explain to Stephanie what had been going on with her, however her agitation was too high. She couldn't stop her anger from bubbling over.

"It's like living with a ten-year-old. How many times do you need to be told not to leave your shoes there?"

"Last time I checked, I live here too. I'm sorry that my stuff seems to offend you so much." Stephanie stormed past her into the kitchen and grabbed a beer from the fridge. She took a swig, then said, "I knew this would be a bad idea. I should have bought the cottage when I had the chance." She finished off the beer in two big gulps, slammed the empty bottle onto the counter, and headed off in the direction of her own bedroom.

Meredith jumped when she heard the door slam. She sat down at the dining table and rested her head on her hands. She knew Stephanie didn't mean what she had said, that she was just reacting to Meredith's bad mood, but the words still stung. She didn't know how long she sat there until Stephanie came back into the room. She was nervous, Meredith could tell. She kept running her hand through her short hair, looking everywhere else but at Meredith. Eventually, she sat down opposite her at the table, resting her hands on the surface.

"I'm sorry I left my shoes by the door. I guess I'm not used to living with somebody, and usually I just leave my stuff wherever. I need to start thinking of you more."

Meredith shook her head. It was just like Stephanie to take the blame for this. After all, she had been taking the blame her whole life. Meredith didn't want her feeling the same way with her. She needed to put this right, she needed to tell her.

"Steph, this is your home now and you have every right to put your things wherever you want. I want you to be comfortable living here and I'm sorry for snapping at you, not just today, but all week." She paused as she gathered her thoughts, trying to think of the right way to tell her about the anniversary, but she couldn't find the words. Instead, she reached across the table and took Stephanie's hands in her own. "Please forgive me."

Stephanie stared at her for a long while and Meredith could see the indecision in her eyes. It was clear Stephanie wanted to press her further, however, she must have decided against it,

"Of course, I forgive you. I will try and be more thoughtful as to where I leave my things."

Meredith wanted to say more, to try and make her understand what was going on but she couldn't. Instead, she just nodded, stood from the table, and went into the kitchen to grab a glass of wine.

"Would you like a glass?" she asked Stephanie.

"Nah, I'm good. I'm going to grab a shower and then we can decide what to have for dinner."

Meredith watched Stephanie leave the room again, glad they were at least trying to get back to normal, but also knowing she was a coward. She had always been able to talk to Stephanie, and now should be no different. She couldn't help but wonder why she couldn't do it this time. She poured some more wine and opened the fridge, trying to find something nice to eat even though she didn't really have an appetite right now. She hoped she could deal with this and not keep taking it out on Stephanie.

†

"I don't know what is going on with her, Fiona," Stephanie said into her mobile phone as she stood in line at the supermarket. It had been three days since the argument about her shoes, and although they both had tried to move past it and act normal with each other, Stephanie could tell there was still something bothering Meredith. She had tried to talk to her about it, but Meredith always said she was fine, for Stephanie to stop worrying. That was asking a lot because Stephanie always worried about Meredith, she couldn't help it.

They had run out of milk and some other ingredients, so Stephanie had offered to go out and pick some up while Meredith started preparing the steaks for dinner. The issues that Meredith was obviously facing were wearing heavily on Stephanie's mind. She thought about ringing Joe to see if he could help but knew he would only give her shit for moving in so soon, so she rang Fiona instead.

"Have you tried talking to her about it?"

"Yes, a few times. But she just says everything is fine and I know she is lying to me. I can't help but think maybe she is having regrets about me being here."

Fiona chuckled. "You're kidding, aren't you? When you were both here it was clear to see how much she loved you.

You know this. So, whatever is going on with her I imagine it has nothing to do with you or your relationship."

Stephanie was silent for a few moments as she tried to recall anything that might be upsetting Meredith. The only thing she could think of was the words Kathleen had said to her. Could that be the reason why she was so off with Stephanie recently? She shook her head. They had already spoken about Kathleen and Stephanie knew Meredith had gotten past that, or so she claimed. Stephanie let out a frustrated breath. She could stand here all day trying to come up with reasons why Meredith was so off, but until Meredith decided she wanted to talk to Stephanie about it, there was nothing she could do. She would just have to make do with Meredith's outbursts.

"I love her too, and as much as it's driving me crazy, she's hurting over something, I know I have to wait until she comes to me. No matter how much I try and talk to her, she just blows me off." Stephanie unpacked her basket on the conveyor belt and slowly moved down the line. "Anyway, how are things with you and Joe? How is he getting on at the gallery without me?"

"He's doing okay, although he did say the other day that he is looking forward to you coming up and looking at the accounts. I told him I would try and help him, but he said he'd rather wait for you. I get the feeling he doesn't trust me with it all."

"I doubt it's that. We got into a routine of things there, and you know Joe, it takes a lot for him to make a change."

"Yeah, well, I think he's just using it as an excuse to wait for you as he misses you so much."

"It's only been a few weeks, but yeah, I miss you guys too." Stephanie reached the checkout and the cashier began scanning her products through the till. "I've got to go, I'm being served."

"No problem. Call me anytime if you need anything. I hope you manage to work things out with Meredith."

"Thank you. I'm sure it will be fine. I'm going to give her some more time to see if she speaks to me about it. I just hope she doesn't have second thoughts about us."

†

Later that night they were lying in bed together. They were in the usual position, Stephanie laying on her back, holding Meredith in her arms. Stephanie wasn't sure what had awoken her, however, it didn't take long to realise that it was Meredith's hand stroking her breast that was rousing her from sleep.

"Meredith? What are you doing?" she whispered. Meredith didn't give any indication she heard Stephanie as she continued her ministrations. Stephanie couldn't help but flinch as the same hand trailed down her stomach and cupped her intimately. She squirmed as Meredith's hand was working its way under her sleep shorts. "Hey, wait a minute. Slow down."

"I need you."

Meredith's voice was roughened by sleep and it sounded sexy as hell to Stephanie. As much as she wanted to be with Meredith, she knew this was wrong. She knew neither one of them was ready for this so she tried to push her away. She took hold of her shoulders and pushed, but Meredith was too eager, too insistent, and pinned her down by pressing her body weight on top of her. She took her mouth in a bruising kiss and it sent Stephanie's hormones soaring. She couldn't help but kiss her back, and as her blood pumped hard through her veins, she felt herself grow wet.

"Please, Steph. Make love to me. Make it go away."

Stephanie could hear the desperation in her voice and she knew she had to stop this. Something was going on and this was not the right time to be doing this. She knew Meredith would regret it in the morning. Using all the strength she could muster, she bucked her hips and managed to flip Meredith over onto her back. She straddled her waist and pinned her wrists above her head.

"Meredith," Stephanie shouted, trying to break through Meredith's resolve. Her eyes were wide, her pupils nearly black. She struggled underneath Stephanie, lifting her head off the pillow, trying to capture Stephanie's breast with her mouth. "Meredith. Stop!"

The harshness of her voice must have penetrated through as Meredith stopped struggling and the passion that Stephanie saw was replaced with fear. She instantly let go of her wrists and climbed off her, not wanting to scare Meredith any more than she so clearly was.

Their breathing was ragged and Stephanie asked, "Are you okay?"

Meredith looked at her and her eyes filled with tears. "I am so sorry. I just wanted it to go away. Why can't I be over this yet?"

Stephanie gathered her in her arms and held her close while Meredith wept. Clearly, she was still struggling with everything that had happened with West and Stephanie didn't know how to help her.

"Do you think maybe you need to go back to your counselling sessions?" She asked cautiously. She herself was pretty much over it. She was not a captive as long as

Meredith had been, and he hadn't tortured her as much. Stephanie had gone to a few sessions with her own counsellor and found them useless, as she knew they would be. Knowing West was going to trial meant he could no longer hurt anyone. It was clear, however, that he had gotten into Meredith's head, and as much as she had improved over the last few months, there were still things going on. There was a good chance Meredith might never get over it. Stephanie was okay with that. She would help as much as Meredith needed or wanted, and she would never think of her as broken. But for her own sake, Meredith needed to find a way of coping with it. More counselling was all Stephanie could think of.

"I hate how much he has ruined my life. He's going to go to prison, yet I still can't let go of what he did to me. I'm worried I'll never be normal again."

"Of course you're normal. We had some horrendous things happen to us, and that isn't something you can easily get over. Meredith, you were there for eight months. You went through a hell of a lot of torture and mind games. I'm sorry, but I don't think this is something you can just forget."

Meredith pulled away from her and wiped the tears from her face. "You seem to have managed to forget it, why can't I?"

"You know how I was back then. I was closed off to every feeling and emotion. I blocked out the things he did to me and stuffed them away so they couldn't hurt me. My way isn't exactly the healthiest way of dealing with it, but it works for me. You're more sensitive than I am, you were there a hell of a lot longer. It's going to take time. But I promise you, we will get through this."

Meredith lay down, pulling the duvet up to her neck. "I'm sorry I accosted you like that. I just wanted the pain to go away."

Stephanie snuggled down into the duvet as well and pulled Meredith into her arms, kissing her forehead. "Never apologise for wanting me. You had me pretty wound up there for a few minutes." She kissed her forehead again and gently rubbed Meredith's back, lulling her into sleep. She lay there awake for a long time after thinking of ways she could help, and ways she could kill Jameson West.

CHAPTER TWENTY-TWO

Meredith stood at the sink swilling out her coffee cup. She jumped when a pair of hands touched her shoulders and lips pressed to the back of her neck. Without thinking, she threw up her elbow, connecting to the jaw of the person behind.

"Ow! Shit, Meredith. That hurt."

She spun around and was dismayed to see Stephanie standing there rubbing her rapidly swelling face.

"Oh God, Steph. I didn't realise it was you."

"Who on earth did you think it would be?"

Meredith went to her and gently caressed her cheek. "I'm so sorry. My mind was elsewhere. Let me get you some ice." She went to the freezer and pulled out the ice tray, then rummaged around in a drawer to find the bag to put the cubes in. She was shaking, on the verge of hyperventilating, her breath coming in quick gasps. She had been thinking about what she had tried to do last night, feeling ashamed for forcing herself on Stephanie. Meredith hadn't heard her walk up behind her. This whole thing with Jameson West was slowly driving her insane. All she wanted was to get back to normal and have a regular relationship with Stephanie, without the events of the last year playing in her mind.

She put the ice cubes in the bag and then guided Stephanie into a chair. Stephanie's eyes were guarded. Meredith could tell she was wary. Stephanie wouldn't quite meet her gaze, her head lowered. Meredith couldn't believe she had elbowed her in the face. Stephanie was the last person she wanted to hurt. This was just another reason why she wished she had never gotten that damn flat tire. If she hadn't got out of the car, he would have never been able to take her. Then the realisation dawned on her. He must have planned it, the kidnapping. It would be a rather strange coincidence that her car happened to break down right where he was waiting to kidnap somebody.

Meredith slumped to her knees in front of Stephanie and whispered, "Oh my God."

Stephanie's gaze connected with hers and Meredith could see the worry on her face.

"What is it?" Stephanie asked.

Meredith shook her head, not wanting to talk about it. It was bad enough she hit her in the face and accosted her last night. She didn't want to add to any more of Stephanie's worries by talking about the day she was taken. She still hadn't mentioned the anniversary that was coming up in a few days, and discussing it now, when her nerves were so frazzled, wasn't something she wanted to deal with.

"Nothing, I can't believe I hit you so hard. Your face is already beginning to bruise." Meredith placed the bag of ice against Stephanie's jaw.

Stephanie furrowed her brow, knowing Meredith was lying to her. She took Stephanie's hand and placed the ice pack in it. She stood and turned her back to Stephanie, gazing out the kitchen window.

"Look, Meredith, I'm not sure what is going on here, but it's pretty obvious there is something you're not telling me. You've been snappy for weeks and you always look lost in thought. Is it me? Do you want me to leave, but don't know how to tell me?"

Meredith spun around and sank to her knees again. The worry on Stephanie's face wasn't hard to miss. She placed her hands on her thighs and gently rubbed. "Of course not. I'm sorry if I made you think that, but please believe me, you being here is the best thing ever to happen to me and I never want you to go. I love you."

Stephanie blew out a breath and quickly looked away. "Then why won't you talk to me? I'd do anything to help you."

"I just can't at the minute. I'm sorry." She stood and gently kissed her on the forehead. "I need to go to work for a few hours. I'll see you later."

Without another word, and without looking back, Meredith fled from the kitchen, grabbed her coat and keys, and was out the door.

†

Just after lunchtime, Stephanie was lying on the sofa, resting another ice pack on her face. She still couldn't believe Meredith had run out on her that morning. There was something going on with her and it was driving Stephanie insane, thinking about what it could be. She knew the trial date coming up had thrown her. However, they had always been able to talk about Jameson West, and Stephanie didn't understand why this could be any different. Her only conclusion was that Meredith wanted her to leave but didn't know how to tell her. Although she had said that wasn't true, Stephanie was still unsure.

She sat up, placing the now defrosted ice pack on to the coffee table. Just as she reached for her laptop, there was a knock at the door. Glancing through the peephole, she didn't recognise the woman standing on the other side of the door. She took the chain off and opened it wide.

"Can I help you?" The woman was about five feet six, with thick auburn hair brushing her shoulders.

"You must be Stephanie. I'm Carrie, a friend of Meredith's."

"Oh yes, she's told me about you. Please come on in." Stephanie stepped aside so Carrie could enter. "Meredith isn't here at the moment. She's had to go to work."

Carrie turned around and faced Stephanie. Her eyes went wide and she gasped.

"That's okay, I just popped by on the off chance she was here. What happened to your face?"

Stephanie's hand automatically went up to the bruise in question and she could feel her cheeks flush red with embarrassment. "Meredith accidentally caught me with her elbow this morning." At Carrie's raised eyebrows, she rushed on, saying, "I think I may have scared her. I came up behind her to give her a morning hug and I guess she wasn't expecting it. Her mind was elsewhere."

"Well, that's hardly surprising considering it's the anniversary tomorrow."

"What anniversary?"

Carrie's eyes went wide again, and Stephanie knew in an instant that Carrie knew why Meredith had been distant and snappy recently.

"What's going on?"

Carrie rubbed her forehead, indecision written on her face. "I'm sorry, but it isn't my place to say. I assumed she talked to you about it since she said she was going to."

"Talk to me about what?"

"I really think you should talk to Meredith about this." She tried to sidestep Stephanie, but Stephanie was too quick and blocked her passage to the door.

"Tell me," Stephanie demanded as she grabbed Carrie's shoulders. Her voice was harsh, she knew this, but she didn't care about coming off as a bitch. She needed to know what was going on with Meredith and this was the only way.

"Tomorrow is the fifteenth of October. It's been exactly twelve months since Meredith was kidnapped."

Stephanie dropped her arms from Carrie and walked backwards, not stopping until her knees hit the sofa, then she collapsed onto it. "Oh my God, I can't believe I forgot."

Stephanie rested her head in her hands, feeling like the world's worst girlfriend. The kidnapping was the worst thing ever to happen to Meredith and was the thing that brought them together. If anybody should have remembered the date, it should have been her.

"Well, that explains why she has been so distant lately."

Carrie placed her handbag by the front door and then came to sit by Stephanie, placing her hand on her knee. "It's okay, I forgot the date as well. She wanted to talk to you about it, about how she's been feeling, but she didn't know how. I guess with it being the anniversary, it has brought up all of the bad emotions."

"We have always talked about everything. That was one of the main reasons our attraction grew so quickly. I can't believe she couldn't talk to me about this."

"Well, now you know. The question is, what are you going to do with this information?"

CHAPTER TWENTY-THREE

Meredith arrived home a little before five o'clock. Going to work that day had been a good distraction from everything she had been feeling. It was bad enough trying to cope with the anniversary of the kidnapping, however, trying to force herself on Stephanie the night before, and hitting her this morning, had pushed her over the edge. She had managed to get quite a lot of work done and that was the only plus side of this whole debacle. During a short lunch break, she had gone for a walk to clear her head, to sort through her feelings regarding the kidnapping. She was still unsettled by it all, but the all-consuming fear she had about it had dissipated. In the end, all she could do was focus on the positive. The positive being that Jameson West was locked up and she was free to pursue her life with Stephanie. She would start by apologising to her for being an asshole.

Meredith opened the front door and the first thing to hit her senses was the smell of roast chicken. The lights in the lounge were dimmed and soft piano music came from the stereo. She closed the door, and then placed her raincoat and shoes in the closet. She chuckled to herself when she noticed three pairs of Stephanie's trainers lined up perfectly.

"Steph? Are you here?" She walked farther into the apartment as Stephanie rounded the corner of the kitchen, wiping her hands on a tea towel. She looked freshly showered, her hair still slightly damp, and her cheeks had a glow about them. She looked delicious.

"Hey, Meredith."

Before she could say anything more, Meredith grabbed hold of her and hugged her tightly, kissing her fiercely on her lips, careful not to hurt the swelling that was still prominent on her cheek.

"Not that I'm complaining, but what was that for?"

"I am so sorry. For everything." Meredith took hold of her hands and gently rubbed her thumbs over her knuckles. "We need to talk."

"It's okay. I know what day it is tomorrow."

Meredith looked away, not wanting her to see the shame she felt. Stephanie lifted her hand and rested it on her cheek, turning her head up to face her.

"Please don't worry. Everything is going to be fine."

Stephanie took her hand and led her to the dining table. She sat her down and kissed her on the forehead. Meredith noted how nicely the table was set for two. Stephanie had obviously found her good china, and a small bunch of daisies sat in the middle of the table with a candle softly burning on either side. Everything looked perfect, and the sight of it broke her heart.

"Dinner will be about another ten minutes," Stephanie said. "Would you like a glass of wine while we wait?"

"Yes, please." Meredith's voice came out in a whisper, Stephanie kissed her on the forehead again, and then went in search of the wine.

Stephanie came back into the room and poured them each a glass of Merlot.

"I hope you don't mind, I have also run you a bubble bath and lit some candles in there. By the time we've eaten it should be just the right temperature for you to get in and have a nice soak. And then I was hoping afterward we could cuddle up in bed and watch a movie or talk or whatever you want."

Meredith smiled. Stephanie looked nervous as hell and she could only guess at what she might be thinking right now. She had taken great lengths to make the perfect evening for them both. The way she wanted to take care of Meredith warmed her heart. She laid a hand on Stephanie's forearm, running her fingers down her soft skin until she entwined her fingers with Stephanie's.

"This is perfect, thank you. And I really am sorry for everything."

Stephanie crouched down, resting her hands on Meredith's knees. "You have nothing to apologise for. I'm the one who is sorry for not remembering what day it is tomorrow. I want tonight to be relaxing for you and if you want to talk about anything we can, or if you just want to snuggle and sleep, we can do that, too. I love you, Meredith, and I don't want you to hurt anymore."

Meredith's breath hitched, and she swallowed hard at Stephanie's sweet words. She was such an amazing person. No matter how many times Stephanie said she didn't feel things the way others did, Meredith knew she had never met a more open, caring, and sensitive person in the world, and she knew she didn't deserve her.

"I love you too," Meredith whispered. "Now feed me, woman." They both laughed as the tension was broken. Before Stephanie stood, Meredith kissed her hard on the lips, enjoying the reconnection of their souls.

†

Later that evening they were curled up in bed together. The television was on with the volume turned down low and the lights were off. The blue light from the TV cast a soft glow over the bedroom. Meredith was lying in Stephanie's arms, and she felt contented. Dinner had been delightful, and the bubble bath had relaxed her tired muscles, and now she felt warm and satiated. Stephanie had been attentive to her all evening, and Meredith felt even guiltier for the way she had been recently. It didn't matter how many times Stephanie tried to reassure her that everything was okay between them, she couldn't help but feel bad for her behaviour. The conversation between them had been pleasant, with no mention of Jameson West or the anniversary tomorrow.

"Thank you for this evening," Meredith said as she gently drew patterns on Stephanie's stomach with her fingertips. "It was very sweet of you." She felt Stephanie kiss the top of her head and her arms tightened around her.

"That's okay. I'm glad you had a nice time."

They settled into a companionable silence as they watched the crime documentary on the television. Meredith glanced at the digital clock on the nightstand and saw it was nearing midnight. She supposed she should be tired, it had been a long day and an extremely relaxing evening, however, she felt a buzz running through her veins. It was almost like a nervous energy pulsing throughout her body, and she realised what she was feeling was arousal. Her breathing quickened and she tried desperately to tamp down her rapidly growing desire to be with Stephanie. This was a new feeling for her. Although they had both expressed their attraction toward each other and said they loved each other, this was the first time since the kidnapping she had felt sexual desire for anyone.

Stephanie must have noticed the change in demeanor and she asked, "Are you okay?"

Meredith shifted on the bed, trying to cool her heated body. She thought about lying, pretending everything was fine, that she wasn't lying here with her body on fire for Stephanie, but she couldn't do that. She had had enough of West ruining her life. It was time to face the truth. She wanted Stephanie. She wanted to touch her, kiss her, make love to her.

Meredith shifted again on the bed, throwing one leg over Stephanie's lower body and leaning up on her elbow. She gazed at Stephanie, not liking the uncertainty in her eyes. Meredith leaned down and gently kissed her on the lips, and without moving a hair's breadth away, she whispered, "Everything is just fine." She kissed Stephanie again with more force, pushing her tongue into Stephanie's mouth. She groaned at the contact as she slid her hand under Stephanie's tank top and gently caressed her breast.

"What are you doing?" Stephanie pulled away, and her intent on stopping Meredith was clear.

"I want to make you feel good, I want to make love to you." Meredith continued to palm her breast. She kissed her way down Stephanie's neck until she reached the peak of her breast, tonguing her nipple through the thin material of her top. She removed her hand and grasped the hem of the T-shirt, yanking it up and over Stephanie's head. The sight before her took her breath away. Stephanie's breasts were perfect, the skin of her abdomen smooth. All evidence of Jameson West's torture long since healed. "You're beautiful."

Stephanie sucked in a breath, gently cradling Meredith's head in her hands, her fingers tangling in her hair.

"You're killing me here. We don't have to do this if you're not ready."

Meredith silenced her by kissing her hard. After a few moments she released her mouth, and slowly she peeled away Stephanie's sleep shorts. Her mouth watered at the sight before her. She had seen Stephanie naked before, but this was different, way different. Meredith's blood pumped hard through her veins. She had never been so turned on in her life, not even with Kathleen. She roamed her hands over Stephanie, caressing her shoulders, her stomach, and thighs. She lowered her head and did the same with her lips. Stephanie's body undulated underneath her.

"I love you," she whispered.

Stephanie captured her gaze. "I love you too. Please don't stop."

"Never."

Her hand gently cupped Stephanie's sex and gently rubbed in a circular motion feeling her hard clitoris against her palm. Ever so gently she inserted her fingers into the wetness and began thrusting. Stephanie threw her head back into the pillow, thrusting her hips in time with Meredith. She had never seen anything more breathtaking than the pleasure on Stephanie's face. All too soon, Meredith could see she was reaching climax as her thrusts became more urgent and her breathing more ragged. She came calling Meredith's name and the sound sent Meredith's hormones raging.

As Stephanie came down from her orgasm she reached for Meredith, kissing her hard. She began undulating on Stephanie's thigh, her own need reaching an incredible level. Her blood pressure skyrocketed, and she was in danger of her own orgasm overtaking her. Stephanie's hands grasped her waist, her fingertips underneath Meredith's own T-shirt. Without thinking, she grasped Stephanie's hands to stop any further progress, her fear consuming her. Stephanie must have sensed her reticence because she stilled all her motions.

"It's okay, Meredith, I'm not going to hurt you."

Meredith looked down into Stephanie's eyes and saw nothing but love, but she couldn't do it. She shook her head as tears threatened to fall. She needed to come, wanted to come, however, she wasn't ready to be touched. She tried to shake the fear away, but it wouldn't leave her. It was stuck inside her, and no matter how much she trusted and loved Stephanie, she couldn't find a way past the brick wall that had forced itself in front of her. She slammed her eyes shut, keeping the tears inside.

"Look at me," Stephanie whispered.

Slowly Meredith opened her eyes and she couldn't stop the flow of tears rolling down her cheeks.

"It's okay," she repeated. Stephanie gently laid her hand on Meredith's cheek, brushing away the tears.

Seeing the compassion and love crumpled Meredith. She fell forward, collapsing into Stephanie's arms, crying hard. Stephanie pulled her closer still, wrapping her in a tight embrace, murmuring comforting words to her. After a few minutes her crying stopped, and she wiped at the last tears on her cheeks.

"I can't fucking believe this. I was so turned on I thought I was going to explode. I'm sorry I froze."

"Please don't apologise. I could feel how wet you were through your boxers. There's no doubt in my mind of how much you want me. We knew this was going to take time and I'm okay with that." She rolled Meredith over, kissing her gently. "That was the most intense orgasm I have ever had. Thank you." She kissed her again, then pulled the discarded duvet up over their bodies. "Please don't worry about what happened. You will know when you're ready and there is absolutely no pressure from me for a timeline. I love you, I love who you are, and sex isn't everything."

"That's sweet of you to say, but it is important. I want you to touch me. I want you to make me come. I was nearly there, and I thought I was going to die from the need I had for you. I was just overcome with fear."

"It's been a tough few weeks, and it's no wonder you froze considering the date. We'll take our time." A wicked smile crossed Stephanie's face as she waggled her eyebrows. "But any time you want to get frisky with me and give me another earth-shattering orgasm, I'm all for it."

"I may hold you to that." Meredith laughed as she kissed her. She scooted further down the bed and rolled onto her side, allowing Stephanie to spoon her from behind. Her arms came around her waist, and Meredith interlaced their fingers, holding her hands tight to her stomach. She might not have been able to let Stephanie touch her intimately just yet, but she knew it wouldn't be long. Her desire to be with Stephanie was too potent, too hard to resist. And she didn't want to resist, not any longer. She fell asleep with a smile on her face, her mind filled with images of Stephanie as she thrashed around reaching orgasm.

†

Early the next morning, Meredith woke with a smile on her face. Her mind replayed the images of last night. Being that close to Stephanie was wondrous, she had never felt so connected to anybody before in her entire life. She stretched her body under the duvet, and at that moment she realised she was alone, Stephanie was not in the bed. She tilted her head, listening for signs of movement coming from within the apartment. She could just make out noises coming from the kitchen so she went in search of her. She found Stephanie leaning over the stove, and the smell of bacon frying made her stomach growl.

"Hey, beautiful."

Stephanie turned around with a wide smile firmly in place. Meredith walked toward her. "Smells wonderful in here. Is any of that for me?"

"I was going to surprise you with breakfast in bed, but you've kind of ruined it by being up already."

Meredith wrapped her in a hug and kissed her.

"I'm ever so sorry. I'll go back and wait for you." Without waiting for a reply, she gave her a quick kiss and sauntered off into the bedroom. She settled back under the duvet and waited for Stephanie. She came in a few moments later with a tray filled with bacon, eggs, orange juice, and a few of the daisies from last night in a glass of water.

"This is lovely, thank you." Meredith took a bite of bacon and groaned as the salty flavour coated her tongue. "Feel free to do this every day."

Before Stephanie could reply her mobile phone rang. "Hang on a sec." She reached for her phone. "It's Joe."

Meredith watched her surreptitiously while eating her breakfast, her nerves jangling. She saw Stephanie's face pale and her hands shake. Her responses to Joe were noncommittal, just "Aha" and "I see." She hung up a few moments later, and Meredith could tell something was terribly wrong. Stephanie avoided eye contact as she fidgeted with the hem of her T-shirt.

"What is it? Is everything okay?" Stephanie took the tray from her lap and placed it on the bedside table. She sat next to her and gently took her hands. "You're beginning to scare me."

After taking a few deep breaths Stephanie locked eyes with her.

"Joe was getting ready for work and he had the morning news on in the background when the reporter's voice caught his attention. Jameson West is dead."

"What do you mean he's dead?" Meredith sucked in a breath, her eyes unable to focus on Stephanie's.

"Apparently, he was found in his cell last night. He had hung himself. That was all the news reports said, Joe doesn't know anything else."

They sat in silence for a few minutes while Meredith tried to process it all.

"Of all the days he had to do this, he had to do it today. Do you think he remembers it was the day he took me?"

"I don't think he did this because of the anniversary. From what I can gather there were other women there before you. I guess it's just a coincidence."

"Yeah, I guess." Meredith shook her head, trying to clear all the thoughts from her mind. "I'll call Detective Walker and see if she knows anything. I can't believe he did this. Why should he get to take the easy way out while we must live with what he did to us for the rest of our lives? It's not fair."

"I know. I was looking forward to seeing the bastard in jail."

"I'm going to go shower." Meredith threw off the duvet and stood from the bed. She walked away from Stephanie and into the bathroom, locking the door behind her. She splashed cold water on her face, then leaned onto the sink. Last night had been perfect and this morning was set to look the same, but yet again, West had ruined everything. He had tainted the time together with Stephanie, and, if it was possible, she hated him even more than she already did. She was glad he was dead. Hopefully now he would be burning in hell for all the abhorrent crimes he committed against them all.

"Meredith?" Stephanie called from the other side of the door. "You okay?"

She dried off her face and then unlocked the door. Stephanie's worry was palpable. "I'm fine, please don't worry." She wrapped her arms around Stephanie's waist and they hugged tightly.

"It's over," Stephanie murmured into her neck. "We never have to see him again."

Meredith wanted to believe her words, that it was finally over, however, just because he was dead didn't mean she could get on with her life as if nothing happened. The repercussions of her time in captivity weren't that easily healed. It was true that they no longer had to face him in court, but she still had to deal with her scars, physical and emotional. She didn't say this to Stephanie, not wanting her to worry any more than she already did.

†

"So, what did she say?" Stephanie asked once Meredith hung up the phone.

After Meredith had showered and waited for an appropriate time to call Detective Walker, she wanted to find out how West had killed himself. Stephanie had tried to talk her out of making the phone call, not wanting her to be any more upset than she clearly was, however Meredith needed to know. Stephanie hoped that by finding the answers they could move on and begin their life together properly, without Jameson West ruining any more than he already had.

"Apparently, after lights out, he had turned his bedsheets into a noose and hung himself from the top bunk. She said he left a suicide note saying he didn't want to spend the rest of his life in prison and this was the only way out."

Meredith let out a shuddering breath and Stephanie could see she was on the verge of tears.

"Did he say anything else?"

"No, that was it. No mention of feeling sorry for his crimes or admitting guilt, just that he didn't want to spend his life in prison."

"What do we do now?" Stephanie went to Meredith and took her hands in her own, running her thumbs over her knuckles. She watched as Meredith shook her head, her lips forming a thin line.

"Nothing's changed, I suppose. We still have to deal with the things he did to us and try to rebuild our lives."

Stephanie guided Meredith over to the couch, sitting down with her, and placing her arm around her shoulders, holding her close.

"I think we both know I have pretty much dealt with what happened. And before you say anything, I know you think I'm still suppressing my feelings over it, but I'm not. Of course, I still think about being there, and occasionally have bad dreams, but it doesn't affect me on a day-to-day basis. I'm just happy I found you and we love each other. I'm looking forward to our life together." She kissed Meredith's cheek and watched as she smiled.

"You're right, you have dealt with this remarkably, considering what happened there. Hopefully now that he's gone, and we don't have to face the trial, I can get over it sooner rather than later." She shook her head. "But I can't guarantee I'll ever be the same again."

Stephanie cupped her cheeks, tilting her face, making sure they had direct eye contact.

"Meredith, I love you. I love who you are now, and yes, we have some things to work through, but you are the sweetest, kindest, most compassionate, and sexiest woman I have ever known. I didn't know you before all this happened, but I love who you are today." She kissed her hard, trying to make Meredith believe her words through her actions. If she had to spend the rest of her life proving to Meredith that she was everything Stephanie wanted, and that there was nothing wrong with her, Stephanie would. Though Meredith carried physical scars from her time of being tortured, they did not detract from her beauty.

Not wanting to continue talking about West, as she could see this was upsetting Meredith, Stephanie changed the subject.

"I had an email come through yesterday afternoon whilst you were at work, offering me a job interview at the University. It's working in the art department and helping one of the professors there. It's only part-time, but it's something."

"That's amazing. Congratulations." Meredith threw her arms around Stephanie's neck, hugging her tightly.

"Well, I don't have the job yet, so we will have to wait and see."

"Oh, you're definitely getting it, they'd be crazy not to have you."

"I was actually thinking of getting back into painting. I haven't done it for a while and it's something I want to have a go at." Stephanie pulled back from Meredith. She looked away, embarrassed about discussing her art. She knew she was good, but still didn't believe she was as talented as the other artists she admired.

"That's great! Hey, why don't we turn one of the spare rooms into a studio for you?" Her face must have been a picture as Meredith began to laugh. "Why do you look so shocked?"

"I just assumed I would rent somewhere, I didn't expect you to offer something like that."

"Well, you can do that if you want, however we have the space here. It wouldn't take much to clear out some of the boxes in there. You could do with it whatever you please and you won't have to pay any extra money for it."

"Are you sure?"

"I'm positive."

Stephanie kissed her again, putting all the love she felt for Meredith in one, long, languid kiss.

CHAPTER TWENTY-FOUR

"Are you sure you don't mind driving down with it all?" Stephanie said to Joe over the phone.

"No, it's fine. It's silly for you to come all the way up here when we're coming down to see you anyway."

They were discussing bringing the rest of Stephanie's belongings from the storage unit she had rented when she moved to Bristol. Joe had said he wanted to visit her anyway after he heard about Jameson West's death, and it made sense to rent a van and bring her stuff with him.

"Okay, well, as long as you're sure. I'll see you next week."

She hung up, turning around from the lounge window she had been looking out of. Her gaze fell upon Meredith, who was curled up on the sofa, napping. It was late in the evening and they had spent a busy few days clearing out the spare bedroom that she would be using as an art studio.

Stephanie sighed as she thought about the past week. Meredith had done an amazing job of not thinking about West killing himself. Stephanie knew she was using the task of cleaning to avoid dealing with it. She supposed in a way it was a good thing. As much as she loved Meredith, it was hard to see her so distraught all the time. She wanted her to be happy, and she felt inadequate that she was unable to heal her.

Stephanie slowly walked over to the couch, gently sitting on the edge. She placed a hand on Meredith's shoulder, slowly rousing her from sleep. She watched transfixed as Meredith's eyes fluttered open.

"Hey," she whispered.

Meredith smiled and Stephanie fell even more in love with her as she gazed at the sleepy face.

"What time is it?"

"It's a little after seven." Stephanie leaned down and softly kissed her on the lips. "Joe and Fiona confirmed their visit next Saturday. He's fine about driving a van down with all my stuff."

"Oh, that's brilliant. I'm glad you don't need to go back up to York again." The look of fear Stephanie always recognised when Meredith spoke of York or Jameson West was absent, Stephanie sent up a silent prayer of thanks at this small victory.

Meredith shuffled back up the couch into a sitting position. "It'll be nice to see them again. I was thinking maybe we could invite Carrie and Holly over for dinner on one of the nights they will be here. I would quite like my friends to meet your friends."

"That's a wonderful idea. Maybe we can have a game of poker?"

"As long as you and Joe don't cheat."

"Hey! We don't cheat, we're just really good."

"Whatever." Meredith rolled her eyes.

Stephanie lunged forward and began tickling her on her stomach, laughing as Meredith tried to bat her hands away. Stephanie straddled her thighs, pinning her in place, and continued the attack while kissing her. Meredith responded to the kiss and her struggles stopped. Instead, Meredith grabbed hold of her waist and pulled her in closer. Stephanie stopped the tickling and moved her hands into Meredith's thick hair, fusing their mouths together. The feel of her drove Stephanie wild, and if she wasn't careful, they would be in danger of going too far. She started to pull back, but Meredith held onto her tighter.

"Don't stop," Meredith whispered. "Please. I want you."

Stephanie searched her eyes, looking for any sign of hesitance, but found none. They were clear, and her pupils had dilated with her apparent arousal. Stephanie felt her own skin flush as heat raced through her body. She nodded as she lowered her head into a passionate kiss. Her hand found Meredith's breast, and her hips bucking when she groaned. Her need was evident when she pulled off Meredith's shorts and underwear, her scent tickling her nostrils.

"Are you sure?"

Meredith didn't answer, she took Stephanie's hand and guided it to her waiting wetness. As soon as Stephanie's fingers touched Meredith's heat, she was lost. She was so soft. Meredith's eyes were closed, her eyebrows scrunched tight. Her hips pumped hard onto her hand as if chasing Stephanie's fingers.

"Inside me, Steph. Quick."

She did as asked and Meredith's eyes went wide, groaning with what Stephanie hoped was pleasure. She moved with her, slowly going in and out, and it wasn't long after when she felt Meredith's walls clamp around her, her thighs trapping her hand in place. She crested, screaming out Stephanie's name.

As she slowly came down from her climax, Meredith reached for her, kissing with such force it nearly knocked Stephanie off her.

"That was amazing," Meredith breathed between kisses.

Stephanie tried to cool her own arousal, in case Meredith needed to talk. This was a very big step, and she expected the realisation of what they had done would be too much for Meredith to cope with. Stephanie was surprised to see Meredith smiling, her face showing nothing but pleasure and contentment. She looked relaxed, all the tension that had been present for months nowhere in sight.

"Are you okay?" Stephanie asked.

"I'm fine. No, better than fine. That was incredible. I can't believe I waited so long for that." She leaned up and kissed her. "I'm suddenly feeling ravenous." Before Stephanie had a chance to reply, Meredith shot off the couch, grabbed her hand, and pulled her toward their bedroom. "I want to do that again. And again, and again."

†

Meredith woke early the next morning with Stephanie nestled in her arms, not an inch of space between them. They had spent the night making love and it was the most wonderful night of Meredith's life. She had always wondered what it would be like when Stephanie finally made love to her, but the reality of it paled in comparison. She had always thought she would have struggled with the intimacy, and probably would have spent the time fearful and crying, thinking that West had ruined her for life. However, he hadn't even crossed her mind. Stephanie had made her feel desirable, and never once treated her like a victim.

She pulled Stephanie closer, tightening her arms around her waist, letting out a contented sigh. She hadn't meant to wake her, but unfortunately, she did. She heard her murmur a "good morning" then Stephanie turned in her arms.

"Hey."

"And how are you this morning?" she whispered. Stephanie cupped her cheek, her thumb lightly tracing her scar.

"I feel wonderful. That was the best night ever." Meredith could feel her cheeks flush as she thought about the previous night's activities, and she couldn't stop herself from smiling. She could see Stephanie didn't quite believe her, the crease between her eyebrows gave her away. "Honestly, I feel great." She leaned forward and kissed the crease away, trailing her lips over her face and finally landing on her mouth. The kiss was unhurried, more of a kiss of reacquaintance than raging passion, but it was the sweetest, most loving kiss Meredith could have asked for.

Pulling back, she said, "You're an amazing woman, Stephanie. I have never felt so loved in my life. Thank you."

"Please don't thank me for loving you. It's not like I had any choice. You're a hard woman not to love."

They rearranged their bodies and settled in to catch a few more hours of sleep. As Meredith drifted off, thoughts of their future swirled through her mind. She didn't know what would be in store for them both, but the one thing she was certain of was that they would be together. It would probably take her a long time to fully recover from her ordeal with West, if ever, but with Stephanie by her side she knew she could achieve anything.

For the first time in a long while, Meredith was looking forward to the future. She wanted to get back into meeting clients out in the field, as she realised she missed that aspect of her job. She was excited to note the thought didn't terrify her like it had in the past. She also hoped that Stephanie could settle things with her father, and finally not blame herself for her mother's death. She had spent too many years closing herself off from people because of her father's horrible words, and Meredith knew it was time she let go of that guilt.

"I can hear your brain working from here," Stephanie murmured. "We're supposed to be sleeping."

"Sorry. Just thinking how lucky I am." Meredith kissed Stephanie's shoulder and settled more firmly into her arms.

"We're both lucky. I love you."

"I love you."

The End

ABOUT THE AUTHOR
A

SAMANTHA HICKS

I am currently working toward my bachelor's degree in art and humanities, and when I am not writing or studying, I can be found with a pencil in my hand drawing pictures of wildlife, pets, and plenty of monkeys. (I love monkeys!) I have quite a few tattoos, and love getting out on my road bike or playing golf, weather permitting. I am currently single and have fallen in love many times with the characters I read about in books by so many terrific authors. It is these stories that have inspired me to write down my own characters that have taken up residence in my head, clamouring to have their own love stories told. My biggest fears are heights and horses and I plan to one day conquer them both. I have a passion for reading, preferring it to almost anything, and hope to one day settle down by the beach.

OTHER AFFINITY BOOKS

<u>Calling Home</u> by Jen Silver
Sarah Frost enjoys her dream job as director of the Frost Foundation making her home at one of their writers' retreats, The Lodge on the Lake. Galen Thomas, taking an extended break from her vet's practice arrives at the island to fill the post of handy person. The island idyll is soon undermined by the revelation of events from forty years earlier, threatening the lives and loves of Sarah, Berry, and Galen. Calling home and what they now call home—all are affected by the disturbing legacy from the past.

<u>Reach of the Heron</u> by Angela Koenig
After an automobile accident takes the lives of her parents and nearly her own, Arkadia O'Malley faces a painful recovery. As she seeks custody of her younger sister, Rini,

she must also contend with the obstruction of Irish law. When Rini is moved from a harsh orphanage to one of the notoriously cruel Magdalene homes, Arkadia's efforts to reunite with her sister are aided by powerful women from this reality as well as from Elsewhere.

From Wind and Water by Laura Kovack
The Seventh Kingdom is surrounded by the Lands of Earth, Fire, Water and Wind. All but Earth have rulers. When a new enemy threatens all of the Lands, it is imperative to find the last ruler of Earth. Morgayne, ruler in Land of Water and Ventus, ruler of Land of Wind, form a tentative yet skeptical relationship—everything depends on them. Will that tie survive the battles ahead? Will they allow or deny their feelings in this fantasy adventure that will have you urging them on to victory on all fronts.

The Book Addict by Annette Mori
From award-winning author Annette Mori comes the captivating story of Tanya, a young woman whose life is unremarkable without any friends or lovers. Then she meets Elle, the alluring owner of the new bookstore, The Enchanted Page. Elle looks like she stepped out of a Nordic adventure and Tanya is immediately infatuated with the mysterious woman. Join the colorful characters as they try to right the wrongs created by Elle's fiercest foe. And just maybe, the books won't be the only thing enchanted if Elle allows the magic of love to enter her heart.

Colors of Rage by Nanisi Barrett D'Arnuk
Dr. Kailyn DeKendran, head of the Acoustic Research Department, and her sister Jayanta, are drawn into the fray of

unrest during the election season when the participants can't remember why they are rioting. When Kailyn disappears, family and friends band together to find her. Time is running out, and the riots are getting more violent. Will they find Kailyn before it is too late to put an end to the madness that has overtaken them?

Naomi's Soul by Renee MacKenzie
This second book in the Karst Series picks up the Peace Movement where Kai's Heart left off. Everyone is still struggling to find the balance between reconciliation and guarding. Control must remain in the hands of those working diligently for peace in the war and disease ravaged New America. Warrior Naomi Adams is on a routine mission for the Peace Movement when tragedy strikes her contingent. She will need to dig deep to find the strength to move past the devastating earthquake that has split up her party.

My Starlight by Loryn Stone
If only we could have met sooner...
Orly Kochav likes nerdy things. A huge fan of Japanese animation, cosplay, and playing the bass, she's convinced she can use her natural charisma and swagger to get anything she wants. Including beautiful girls. When her judgmental mother catches her kissing a girl and asks her a hideous question, Orly goes into a state of emotional hiding. Now sixteen, Orly is itching to reclaim her prior life and when a new friend informs her that a secret club dedicated to their favorite Japanese Anime, Lovely Starlight Fighter, is at their high school, Orly thinks she'll be able to slip back into the world of fandom without issue. Until she meets the club's vice president, Danielle Cohen and the rising attraction to her

threatens to make Orly question every choice she's about to make.

True North by Ali Spooner
Cam's story continues as the Gator Girlz business continues to thrive under her leadership, but will self-doubt jeopardize her relationship when Bugsy reveals the family moonshine business to an unsuspecting Luce? Will a devastating injury to Sandy end her career as a gator hunter or will it open a door to love? Join the St. Angelo family for a third adventure to find out more about life, loving, and family in Bayou Country.

The Dream Catcher by Annette Mori
What if all your dreams—the good ones and the nightmares—came to life in the real world?
Heaven is a Dream Weaver, and that is her reality. When she wakes up, she never knows what will greet her or her best friend and roommate, Syl. It could be a sexy stripper or a monster from another dimension. When Syl suggests a Dream Catcher to help her control the dreams, Heaven is wary until she meets the alluring Maya. Between the government and the powerful Dream Catching sisters, time is running out for Heaven. She wonders who she can trust. Can this lovely Dream Catcher protect her or is Heaven truly on her own?

Gator Girlz by Ali Spooner
In the sequel to Diamond Dreams, Cam St. Angelo finished her freshman year on a high. Her softball career is on path. Everything seems to fall in place for Cam and Tab as the new school year and softball season take off. All too soon,

unfortunate events at the home front force Cam to leave college and her softball dreams behind. As always, it's family first.

The Tempest by JM Dragon
Doctor Alana Cameron has dedicated her life to working on the family legacy, a transportation device which will change the world for everyone, called Tempest. Tragedy has dogged the project over the years, causing military intervention. Super soldier Major Denise Tranter, who loyally defends Earth in any way possible, finds herself drawn into the Tempest program. Emotional bonding is not in her remit, although she finds herself inexplicably drawn to Alana.

Trusting Hearts by Samantha Hicks
When successful advertising executive Carrie-Ann Stedman is tasked to train a new hire, she is reluctant. She has never forgiven Holly Fletcher, the newbie, for stealing an important client away from her. Holly doesn't know what Carrie's problem with her is. When the two are thrown together, can they build a working relationship without business getting in the way of the growing attraction between them?

Free to Love by Ali Spooner and Annette Mori
Captain Hillary Blythe loves sailing the ocean. Her journeys along the Atlantic Coast and Caribbean to deliver goods contain many adventures. When she brings a small group of rescued Africans to the Methodist mission on Antigua, challenges to deeply ingrained beliefs arise when devoted Christian, Elizabeth Allen, is drawn to one of the women,

Kia. Will Kia and Elizabeth be free to love among the harsh laws of the land and Elizabeth's struggles with her faith?

Kai's Heart by Renee MacKenzie
The time has come for the Resistance to take back control of New America from the Anointed tyrants. Growing up as the daughter of a Resistance Army General, Kai Brodie's focus is keenly on the upcoming Revolution. So how is it then that she can't take her eyes off the beautiful Anointed guard? Can Kai break free from tradition and find love in the arms of someone her upbringing tells her she should hate? Can she protect her love from those who hunt them? Will Kai and Rachel survive the battle over the fate of their beloved New America?

Diamond Dreams by Ali Spooner
Cameron St. Angelo dreams of playing softball in the College World Series. Earning a scholarship to play ball for her beloved LSU brings Cam one step closer to achieving this dream. When Cam arrives on campus, she joins a family of women who share her love of the sport, and she realizes there is room in her life for another love.

Unconventional Lovers by Annette Mori
Bri and Siera are young women with huge hearts and strong wills; they want nothing more than to find a peaceful and secure space to be themselves. But the world is a harsh place for anyone who is different. Bri's Aunt Olivia is a vet who channels her emotions into her work and her love of Bri. Siera has her Aunt Deb who adores her. Despite their individual battles against hurt, prejudice, and rejection, can these four women find love against the odds?

Affinity
Rainbow Publications

ebooks, Print, Free ebooks

Visit our website for more publications available online.

www.affinityrainbowpublications.com

Published by Affinity Rainbow Publications
A Division of Affinity eBook Press NZ LTD
Canterbury, New Zealand

Registered Company 2517228